MURDER AT THE POLO CLUB

A High Desert Cozy Mystery - Book 4

BY

DIANNE HARMAN

Published by: Dianne Harman
www.dianneharman.com

Interior, cover design and website by
Vivek Rajan
www.RewireYourDNA.com

ISBN: 978-1539480082

CONTENTS

ACKNOWLEDGMENTS

There are three people I want to thank for making my incredible journey as an author possible: my husband, Tom, Vivek Rajan, and you, my reader.

Tom for helping me every step of the way from advice on plots, to elaborate charts showing me what people like best about my books, to a critical eye when it comes time to edit.

Vivek Rajan for his sound advice, his beautiful covers, and his unfailing ability to format my books and make them look good.

And last, but certainly not least, you, dear reader. Without you I wouldn't be a successful author. I so appreciate your taking the time to read my books, review them, and make them bestsellers!

Without the three of you, none of this would have happened, so, from the bottom of my heart, I sincerely thank you!

As you read this book, you may wonder why I've chosen to write about the appraisal of antique and fine art objects. For many years I owned an antique and fine art appraisal business. I was fortunate to be hired by the IRS, judges, lawyers, insurance companies, and high wealth private individuals to place values on items of personal property.

It was and is a fascinating business. Many of the antique and fine art objects described in my High Desert series of books are of the same type and value as the ones I actually appraised. Thought you might like to know that the descriptions of those objects in my books are not fiction.

Win FREE Paperbacks every week!

Go to www.dianneharman.com/freepaperback.html and get your FREE copies of Dianne's books and favorite recipes immediately by signing up for her newsletter.

Once you've signed up for her newsletter you're eligible to win three paperbacks. One lucky winner is picked every week. Hurry before the offer ends!

PROLOGUE

I know I promised Jack I'd quit smoking, but I'm a nervous wreck meeting all of these polo bigwigs. One cigarette can't hurt me, and I'll go behind the barn so no one will see me.

Pia Marshall looked around the barn where the guests were walking from stall to stall admiring Jack's polo ponies while carrying drinks from the two bars set up at either end of the barn. She glanced out at the expanse of carefully landscaped grounds separating Jack's huge desert home from the barn and saw people already lined up at the tables where the caterers had set out massive trays of hot and cold appetizers. The grounds and the barn were swathed in a beautiful blaze of color. It looked like the pictures she'd seen of English manor gardens. Everything was perfect.

Most of the guests were dressed in white pants or slacks imitating what the polo players wore as well as shirts and blouses which reflected the colors of Jack's team, a combination of red, white, and blue. Jack was very patriotic, and he'd adopted the colors of the United States flag when he'd formed his team. Even though he'd explained the game of polo to her a number of times, she'd never seen a live polo game, so she was eagerly looking forward to the beginning of the season. In keeping with his team colors, she wore white silk pants, a blue and white striped blouse, and a red and white Parisian scarf carefully tied in a French knot.

1

Pia had put one cigarette and some matches in the small red, white, and blue handbag that hung from her shoulder by its gold chain before she'd left for the barn, anticipating the need for an emergency smoke break. She told Marty she'd be back in a few minutes, slipped out the wide barn door, and walked behind the barn where she'd be out of sight of the guests. She lit the cigarette and inhaled, feeling better almost immediately. It was the last time she'd feel good.

Suddenly a hand reached from behind her and slapped a cloth against her mouth. She dropped the cigarette and tried to fight off her assailant. She was terrified and breathing deeply which only made the chloroform act faster. Unconscious in moments and with a pre-existing heart condition, death came swiftly. Her attacker released her and her lifeless body slid to the ground. The killer bent down and put out her cigarette, not wanting the lit cigarette to draw anyone's attention, but it was too late. Voices were coming closer. It was time to leave.

CHAPTER ONE

"I suppose it's time for me to get back to reality. Between the wedding and the honeymoon in Hawaii, my thoughts have definitely not been focused on conducting detective work for the Palm Springs Police Department," Jeff said as he grinned at his bride of two weeks. Smiling back at him, Marty (formerly) Morgan, now Combs, heaped some lox and cream cheese on the bagel she was about to eat. Sitting at her feet was Marty's faithful black Lab, Duke, who was hoping she'd drop a scrap of the lox. With Duke's affinity for fish, Marty often wondered if he'd been a cat in a previous life.

"I thought the wedding was fabulous," Marty's sister, Laura, said as the residents of the compound owned by Laura sat in the courtyard sharing a light breakfast before leaving for work.

Laura's significant other of many years, Les, a well-known local artist, reached down and petted Duke. "You have to admit that even though I did a superb job as best man, I think having Duke stand next to the two of you when you said your vows was the highlight of the wedding. I suppose the only thing that would have made it better is if I'd put his pink booties on him, but since he wasn't going outside, I didn't think it was necessary."

"I still can't believe how much food the guests went through at the reception," John, the owner of the popular Red Pony food truck, said. "Max and I worked for two days getting everything ready, and

1

we really thought we'd fixed way too much. As it was, we barely had enough. Given the size of our courtyard, I think having an open house type of reception was much better than having it at a set time. That part worked well, actually, it all worked well."

John looked at his watch and said, "Max and I are catering a big cocktail party at the Rutledge Polo Club tonight. Evidently the owner wants to spark some interest for the upcoming season, so he's invited a lot of the horse owners and big supporters of the sport. I understand it's not only the polo people from around the Palm Springs area who will be attending, but they're coming from as far away as Florida and New York, maybe even farther. Should be an interesting evening."

"Small world," Marty said. "When we came home last night there was a message for me from Laura's boss, Dick, at the insurance company where they work, asking me to appraise two different collections. One is art glass and the other one is art pottery. Here's the coincidence. The owner of the polo club, Jack Rutledge, is getting married in a couple of weeks. His bride-to-be just moved into his huge estate-size home.

"Evidently Jack Rutledge has collected American Art Pottery for years, and his bride-to-be has a huge collection of French and American Art Glass she inherited from her parents. Jack asked Dick's insurance company to insure both collections, but they have to be appraised before the company will issue an insurance policy on them, although they already insure the contents of the house. I have an appointment with them at ten this morning."

"Marty, as much as I'd like to stay here and continue our honeymoon, duty calls, but believe me, although my body may be at the police station the rest of the day, my mind will be back in Hawaii with you!" Jeff said as he leaned over, kissed her goodbye, and headed for the gate leading to the parking area. "See you all tonight."

"Yeah, I'm in the middle of a painting that's captured my attention, so I better get back at it before I lose my momentum," Les said.

"As much as you're getting paid for your artwork these days, I think that's a good idea," Laura said grinning at him. "Anyway, I need to go hold Dick's hand and see what problems his insureds are having today." She stood up and walked over to her home, one of the four houses that surrounded the common courtyard. When Marty's husband decided to divorce her so he could marry his lover over a year ago, Laura insisted she leave her home in the Midwest, come to California, and live in one of the houses in the compound. Considering it had resulted in Marty meeting Jeff, it had been a very good decision!

CHAPTER TWO

Frank Marshall looked at himself in the bathroom mirror of the small apartment he'd rented two days earlier. He was glad his brother had loaned him some money, because there was no way he could have rented an apartment with the token money the state of California had given him when it released him from prison. They even subtracted out the cost of the clothes he'd worn on the bus ride back to Los Angeles.

He'd called his old friend Louie when he'd gotten back in town and asked him for a job. Frank knew he'd have to be careful, since he was on parole. He thought it was kind of funny that the only thing he'd learned in the ten years he'd been in prison was how to sell the drugs smarter, so he wouldn't get caught next time. He also thought how ironic it was that it was easier to buy drugs in prison than it was to buy them on the street. What was a convicted felon with no skills supposed to do to earn money?

When Frank had filled out the application for the apartment, he'd listed a phony home address and told the landlord he'd been taking care of his elderly father who had Alzheimer's for the last few years, and he hadn't been able to work. He said when his father had died he needed to make a fresh start. It hadn't hurt that Frank had seen an elderly man who appeared to be suffering from dementia in the landlord's living room who bore a strong resemblance to the landlord. The landlord gave him the key to the seedy apartment, no questions asked.

He'd met with Louie the night before and still couldn't believe what he'd told him. When Frank suspected he was going to be arrested and probably go to prison he told Louie he wouldn't tell the police where he'd gotten the drugs he distributed. In return, he asked Louie to keep an eye on his wife, Pia, and let him know what she was doing. When he'd been sentenced to ten years in prison for selling methamphetamines and possessing an illegal firearm, she'd told him she was going to divorce him. True to her word, a few weeks later a process server had come to the California prison where he was incarcerated and served him with divorce papers.

He sighed deeply, thinking about how lonely the last few years had been. Pia was the only person he'd ever loved. When his parents had died from drug overdoses while only in their mid-thirties, he'd supported himself from the time he was sixteen doing the one thing he knew how to do, sell drugs. One day when he'd made a lot of money from sales, he decided to treat himself to a nice pair of shoes. He went to an upscale department store in the mall near where he'd been selling the drugs and was waited on by Pia. He still remembered how she looked that day. Her long dark hair and big brown eyes had left him almost breathless. He bought the shoes, and he convinced her to have a drink with him after she got off work at 9:00 that night.

He fell deeply in love with her, but he was smart enough to know that if she found out what he did for a living, he'd never see her again. Frank reinvented himself for Pia. He told her he was employed as a personal assistant for a man who worked erratic hours which explained why sometimes he had to work at night. A few months after he first met her they were married at a wedding chapel in Las Vegas. No one attended the wedding. Pia's family met him once when they came to Los Angeles on a vacation. It was obvious they didn't approve of the marriage. In fact, Pia and her parents had become estranged soon afterwards.

True to his word, Louie had kept Frank up to date on what Pia was doing. He knew her parents had died, and that she'd made a trip back to their home in New Jersey. Louie had also told him she'd driven a U-Haul truck back to Los Angeles, but he hadn't been able to find out what was in it. Louie told him about the men she'd gone out with over the years, but there didn't seem to be a favorite, since she went from one to another. A year ago he told Frank that Pia had been steadily seeing a wealthy Italian, Roberto Battisto, who owned a restaurant in Beverly Hills which catered to the stars. He also told Frank the word on the street was that although Roberto was very discreet, he had strong ties to the Mafia.

A month ago he told Frank that Pia was no longer seeing Roberto, but instead she'd started seeing a wealthy man who owned a polo club in Palm Springs and who'd made his money investing in high tech start-ups in Northern California. Although the man lived in Palm Springs, he drove to Los Angeles several times a week to see Pia.

When Frank arrived in Los Angeles, the first thing he'd done when he got off the bus was call Pia, but her number had been disconnected. He'd taken a cab and gone to her apartment, but she no longer lived there, and no one could give him any information about her. When Frank met Louie last night, he'd asked Louie if he knew where Pia was. Louie had hemmed and hawed and seemed very reluctant to tell Frank anything. Finally, Frank had threatened Louie by telling him it wasn't too late for him to go to the police and tell them about Louie's involvement in drug trafficking.

Just thinking about what Louie had told him the night before caused a fresh wave of red rage to wash over Frank. The angry eyes that looked back at him from the mirror were red with fury. He thought going to prison was the worst thing that could ever happen to him. That was before Pia told him she was divorcing him. He was sure that was the worst thing that could ever happen to him. Now he knew the worst thing that could ever happen to him was to find out the only person he'd ever loved was going to marry one of the wealthiest men in Palm Springs, maybe even in California.

The dream he'd kept alive for all those years while he was in prison had instantly become a nightmare. He knew, beyond the shadow of a doubt, there was no way Pia would ever be his again.

No, Pia would be the wife of some wealthy Palm Springs man who owned a string of polo ponies. Although he wouldn't let himself think it consciously, on some level he knew he'd rather see Pia dead than be married to someone else. A plan began to form in his mind. He wasn't sure exactly how it would come about, but he knew he was capable of doing whatever was necessary to make sure Pia never married the rich polo man from Palm Springs.

Frank walked out of the tiny bathroom and in three strides crossed the room the landlord had referred to as a living room. He picked up his cell phone from the kitchen counter and pressed in some numbers.

"Yeah, it's me. Louie, I need ya' to get somethin' for me. I know ya' got ties all over this city. Ya' do this fer me, and I'll consider us even. No talkin' to the cops, ever. Here's what I need…"

CHAPTER THREE

When Marty had returned Dick's call the evening before, he'd given her directions to the Polo House, Jack Rutledge's home. He explained that the home and grounds were among the most spectacular in the Palm Springs area. The insurance company where Dick and Laura worked specialized in providing coverage for very high-end clients. Marty had been in a number of wealthy client's homes since she'd relocated to Palm Springs, but nothing prepared her for what she saw when she turned into the driveway of the Polo House.

The estate was situated on five acres which, for privacy and security reasons, was entirely enclosed by an eight-foot-high stone and brick wall. The entrance gate led to a security shack where a uniformed guard was on duty 24/7. After passing through the security checkpoint, the lane split in two, one section leading to the main house, barn, and Jack's son's home. The other section led to the polo field which could be seen off in the distance.

Palm trees lined the lane which led to the huge Southwestern style one-story red tiled roof home. The lane ended in a semicircular driveway in front of the massive house. Marty pulled to the far side of it and walked back to the large beveled glass doors which were located in the center of the house. The house appeared to have a main center section and a wing on each side. Even though she'd become somewhat familiar with succulents and cacti from living in the Palm Springs area, she couldn't believe the landscaping of the estate. Huge brightly colored plants were set among different types of grasses. She'd never seen most of the plants and imagined they were as rare and expensive as the collections she was about to appraise.

She rang the doorbell, and the door was quickly opened by a beautiful Mexican woman who appeared to be in her mid-thirties. She wore a tan uniform with a white collar and belt. "May I help you?" she asked.

"My name is Marty Morgan, er, Combs. Sorry, I just got married, and I haven't gotten used to my new name yet. I'm an antique appraiser, and I have a meeting at ten this morning with Jack Rutledge and Pia Marshall."

"Yes, they told me you were coming. My name is Lupe. Mr. Rutledge said to show you into the library. They're next door in the barn. He likes to check on his polo ponies every day."

"Does he have many ponies?" Marty asked as she followed Lupe down a long hall to the library.

"He has sixteen. In addition to the ones he rides, the ponies for the rest of his polo team are also kept in the barn. I'll be back in a moment. May I get you some iced tea?"

"No, thanks," Marty said. She stood in the middle of the huge room, staring in awe at the walls lined with bookshelves. Two of the walls had moveable wooden ladders, so the books on the top shelves could easily be retrieved. Since this was Jack Rutledge's estate, Marty assumed that the books were his. She looked at them a little closer and noticed that about every genre written was represented, and the shelves were filled with what looked to be priceless antique books as well as contemporary novels.

She gasped involuntarily when she noticed a Rookwood lamp on a desk which she judged to be worth thousands of dollars. She'd never seen one that spectacular, even when she'd visited the Rookwood Museum in Delaware.

"I see you recognize that lamp," a male voice said from behind her. Startled, Marty turned to face a tanned handsome older man with a mane of white hair and a petite dark-haired woman by his side, and said, "Yes, that lamp is simply incredible. I've never seen one quite like it."

"I'm not surprised. From what I've been told, there isn't another one like it, and that's what makes it so valuable." He walked over to her and extended his hand. "I'm Jack Rutledge, and this is my fiancée, Pia Marshall. Welcome to the Polo House."

"If your other art pottery and art glass items are anywhere near the quality of this lamp, I'd bet you probably own two of the best collections in the United States."

"I do bet on polo," Jack said, "but never when my team is playing, but that's a bet I won't take. You see, I've been collecting art pottery for years. I was lucky enough to be at the right place at the right time, I sold some start-up high tech companies of mine which allowed me to indulge in my collecting habit and eventually to fulfill my dream of owning a polo facility."

"Well, I, for one, am glad you were able to collect the pottery, or we probably never would have met," the short Italian brown-eyed woman standing next to him said. "If I hadn't gone to the antique show to try and get some idea of what my parents had left me, I wouldn't be standing here right now."

"That you wouldn't," he said smiling indulgently at her. "Mrs. Morgan, I believe that was the name on your business card that Dick gave me, how do you want to go about this?"

"Well, first of all, the name isn't Morgan anymore. I just returned from my honeymoon, and now my name is Marty Combs."

"In that case, I imagine congratulations are in order. Pia and I are getting married in three weeks, and that's the purpose of the appraisal."

"Please, tell me a little more. When I talked to Dick at the insurance company all he said was that I was to appraise an art pottery collection as well as an art glass collection."

"That's true, but there's a little more to it than that. My art pottery collection was appraised several years ago, although I never had it insured. I was just curious what it was worth. What I want you to do with it is update the values listed on it and appraise the pieces I've collected since then, so I can have it insured. Here's the appraisal that was previously done." He handed Marty the appraisal.

She took it from him and glanced at it. "I don't know who did it, but it looks to be quite thorough. Is there any chance I could have a copy of it? I also need to personally see the items listed in the appraisal to make sure you still have all of them, and that they're in the condition as noted in the appraisal."

"Not a problem," Jack said. "I'll walk you through the collection when you're ready to do it. I'd like you to do Pia's collection first. She inherited a number of French and American art glass pieces from her parents who recently passed away. Her mother and father collected the glass for years, but they never had any of it appraised. They didn't trust appraisers, and the items weren't insured. Pia just moved into my house a few days ago, and all of the pieces contained in their collection are still in the boxes Pia packed them in when she brought them out to California in a U-Haul truck.

"We thought the easiest way to do this would be for you to take the pieces out of the boxes and appraise them one by one. When you've finished we'll figure out where we want to put them. By the way, Pia and I have signed a trust agreement, and these pieces are going to be included as part of the trust."

Pia looked at Marty and said, "I'm sorry, but I have no idea what's even in the collection. That's why I was at the antique show. I realize I should know something about them if I'm going to own them."

"If we're going to own them," Jack said smiling. "Kind of old school, but what's mine is yours and yours is mine."

"Excuse me, Mr. Rutledge," Lupe said walking into the room. "There's a man at the front door, Kevin Sanders, and he says he needs to talk to you. He said to tell you it is very important."

Jack Rutledge flushed, and an angry look passed over his face. "That no-good…"

"What's this about, Jack? I've never heard of him, and I've never seen you like this," Pia said with a look of concern on her face.

"I better go talk to him. Let's just say if there's one person I hate in the polo world, he's the one," Jack said as he turned and followed Lupe out of the room.

CHAPTER FOUR

"I know, Mom. I can't believe it either," Jensen Rutledge said, "I found out a few days ago. I wanted to be the one to tell you, so you didn't read about it in the paper or hear about it from one of your so-called friends."

"I really never thought this would happen," Debbie Rutledge said in a teary voice. "I know we grew apart, and he never forgave me after he found out I was having an affair. That's why he divorced me, but as hurt as he was by that, it never occurred to me he'd remarry. Have you met her?"

"Yes. She moved in two days ago. Mom, she's nothing like you. You've got more class in your little finger than she has in her whole body. I don't understand what he sees in her."

"Tell me what you know about her," Debbie said, struggling to keep her voice under control.

"Well, she's Italian. She has long jet black hair and big brown eyes. I suppose Dad finds her attractive, but I'd think she'd have a little grey in her hair at her age. Probably uses a bottle to keep her hair that color."

"Sweetheart, hate to say it, but most women my age use the bottle to cover up a few gray hairs. Speaking of age, how old do you think she is?"

"She's younger than Dad. I'd say she's probably in her late forties, maybe early fifties. She's short, and I guess I'd have to say she has a nice figure."

"What's her background? Has she been previously married?"

"I don't know. Neither she nor Dad has mentioned what kind of work she did while she lived in Los Angeles or if she'd ever been married."

"What's her name? I'm going to Google her and see if anything comes up," Debbie said, her voice much stronger now that the initial shock of what her son had told her was over.

"Pia Marshall. That's all I know. Hold on, Mom. I'm going into the kitchen and get a beer. I'll be back in a minute. Why don't you Google her while I'm getting my beer?" Jensen put the phone down and looked across the polo grounds at the barn and his father's luxurious home. Most people would say that Jensen's home was simply a smaller model of his father's home and quite luxurious in its own right. It was several hundred yards from the main house and in close proximity to the polo grounds.

Being the manager of a polo club and polo grounds owned by your father isn't a bad gig, Jensen thought. *Sometimes I think it's all about being born to the right parents, and I was lucky enough to win the lottery.*

With a freshly opened beer in his hand, he walked back into his office and picked up his phone. "Find out anything, Mom?" he asked.

"Jensen, not many things shock me at this point in my life, but I have to say I've never been as shocked as I am at this momen

"What do you mean? What did you find out?"

"She worked as a shoe clerk in Los Angeles, but that's not the worst of it. If you're not sitting down, you might want to. Her ex-husband was convicted of drug trafficking and spent ten years in prison. I Googled him and found out he just got out of a California prison. She's a nobody. I can't understand what your father sees in her. I'll bet she's a gold digger. If you don't want to be working as a shoe clerk yourself down the road, you better do something to stop the marriage, because your new stepmother is an absolute nothing who was previously married to a felon. I can't believe what your father's doing.

"Since he seems to have lost his senses, I'll bet he'll leave everything to her, and the polo grounds and the home you've shown me pictures of will be nothing but a nice memory for you. Since she's obviously younger than he is, he'll probably go first, and she'll get everything, although what a shoe clerk would know about owning a polo club and polo grounds is beyond my imagination," Debbie said snidely. "Do you know if they've signed wills or created a trust? You've got to protect your interests as well as mine. I'm still getting alimony from your father. If he dies, I'm sure I'll never get another dime."

"I know Dad's attorney came to the house yesterday, because I recognized his car, but I have no idea what took place. Mom, you're really making me nervous."

"Jensen, you better be nervous. Let me be very clear about this. If they get married and he dies first, which common sense says he will, your days as the manager of the Rutledge Polo Club are through. I doubt she'd keep you on out of the largesse of her heart. Since she probably doesn't know anything about polo, I'll bet she'd sell all of it and move back to Los Angeles. With what she'd get from your father's estate, she could buy just about any mansion she wanted in Beverly Hills."

"Mom, I need to sign off. Dad's having a big cocktail party here tomorrow night, and he's put me in charge of making sure the barn and the grounds are spotless. The crew and I have quite a bit more to do. Let me think about this, and I'll get back to you."

"Do that, Jensen, but you better figure out some way to keep their marriage from happening."

*****

In the middle of the night Jensen awoke with a start, his mind having devised a plan while he slept. He looked at his clock mentally calculating how many hours he had until the store opened. He wanted to be the first one there and needed to be back at the house as soon as possible. With the cocktail party this evening, there were a number of last minute things that needed to be done. He smiled, knowing that the problem his mother had described could be taken care of rather easily.

CHAPTER FIVE

"Marty," Pia said, "I know you must think I'm an idiot for not knowing how much my things are worth or even what they are, but I left the family home many years ago and moved to Los Angeles. My family lived in New Jersey. My father owned several supermarkets, and my mother was a lawyer. They did very well financially, and it allowed them to indulge in their passion of collecting art glass."

"Not at all, Pia, a lot of children have no idea that what their parents own may have some significant value."

"Well, it's a little more than that in my case. My parents didn't approve of the man I married, and we were estranged for many years. As it turned out, they were right. After I divorced him, my parents and I reconciled a few years later. My father died shortly after that, and then recently my mother died. My sister lived near my parents, but for some reason I was the recipient of their art glass collection and their house. I was also named by them as the executor of their estate. My sister was not very thrilled that I essentially got everything. I've often wondered if my parents felt guilty about those years of estrangement."

"Who knows? Families are funny, but it looks like you've started a new life, and from what I've seen, it's going to be a very good life," Marty said.

"Just between you and me, I sure hope I don't do something to embarrass Jack. He's a wonderful man, and I can't believe how lucky I am that he loves me and wants to marry me. I'm a little nervous about it because I've never been around anything like this," Pia said gesturing wide with her arms. "I often had to work two jobs to make ends meet. My husband's work was unsteady, so I was never exposed to dinner parties or polo. This is a completely different world for me. For instance, I don't have a clue how to be the hostess at a dinner party, although tonight I'm going to be tested as the hostess of a large cocktail party."

"Pia, it really is a small world. I live in what could loosely be called a compound. There are four houses which surround a large courtyard. One of the men who lives there is a chef, and he happened to mention at breakfast this morning that he's going to be the caterer for your cocktail party tonight. Since I've eaten more meals of his than I can count, I can assure you the one thing you don't need to worry about is the food that will be served. He's a genius when it comes to cooking."

"Good. By the way, I have a favor to ask of you. I just moved here from Los Angeles two days ago. As Jack mentioned, we met at an antique show in Los Angeles and continued to see one another, but other than Jack's son and my sister, who arrived unexpectedly last night, I don't know anyone who will be coming to the cocktail party tonight. I'd feel a lot better about it if you would come as my guest. At least that way I'd know one friendly face in the crowd of strangers."

"I've never been to anything that has to do with polo, but I'd love to come," Marty said. "Thanks. I'll call my husband, who's a detective with the Palm Springs Police Department, and see if he can join me. Do you think it will be alright with Jack?"

"Of course," she said laughing. "He just wants me to be happy, but who wouldn't be happy living in a beautiful mansion like this? My collection is in my half of the wing on this side of the house, down this hall."

Marty realized that the two wings of the house she'd seen when she arrived extended back on each side of the central part of the house and flanked a large swimming pool and outdoor entertainment area.

"I can't believe I actually have all this room. Jack said I can change the furniture if I want to, but I think the decorator did a good job. What do you think?" Pia asked as she opened the door to her suite.

"It's beautiful," Marty said looking at the tastefully decorated sitting room with Navajo rugs scattered on the highly polished tile floor, old chests that served as storage containers and tables, as well as couches which had been covered in bright Southwest colors, reminiscent of the peach, pink, and purple colors of the desert sunsets. Large white wooden shutters opened out onto the enormous pool and brightly striped cabanas next to it.

"Here's my bedroom. It's decorated pretty much the same. My suite is bigger than the entire apartment I lived in for years in Los Angeles. There are times I feel like I grabbed the golden ring on the carousel. Look at this bathroom. It has everything anyone would ever need, and the walk-in closet is enormous."

"Looks to me like Jack designed it with you in mind. This really has been decorated beautifully. What's this?" Marty asked, pointing to a needlepoint sign on the door that read, "Welcome."

Pia smiled abashedly. "I know it sounds silly, but I want to keep the romance alive when we're married. I remember reading one time that if a woman was lucky enough to have her own bedroom, she should have a sign on the door that specified when someone was welcome. That way you'd always look good for the person you were trying to impress. I don't want Jack to be disappointed he married me."

"I'm no psychologist, but from what I've seen of Jack, I don't think that's going to be a problem," Marty said. "Did you do the needlepoint on it?"

"Yes. You'll notice a number of pillows on the couch and on the bed. I've done all of them. I'm a lousy cook, gardening doesn't excite me, I know very little about art, music, or polo, but I'm very good at needlepointing."

"Pia, I think you're going to be a very quick study. I see a number of boxes at the far end of the sitting room. I'm assuming your parent's art glass collection is in them."

"Yes. I went back to my parent's home and arranged for the house to be sold. Surprisingly enough, there wasn't much money in the estate. I didn't feel comfortable taking both the art glass collection and the proceeds from the house, so I gave my sister the money from the sale of the house, since she was the one who'd really taken care of my parents for the last few years. They spent pretty much everything they had on this collection. I have no idea what it's worth, but based on the fact they both had successful careers, I would think there must be some good pieces in it."

"There's only one way to find out. I need to get a few things out of my car before I start. Why don't you take the pieces out of the first box, so I can get started? What does Jack think of your collection?"

"He's only seen a couple of the pieces. I boxed them up, and as I said, I drove a U-Haul truck from New Jersey to my apartment in Los Angeles. My apartment was very small, so it was easier to just keep them boxed up, and I really didn't have anywhere to put them. This has all happened pretty fast. Jack and I only met two months ago, but like he said, at our age what are we waiting for? I was a shoe clerk in a large department store, so I gave notice and moved in with Jack a few days ago. It's been a whirlwind with lawyers, moving my things, planning the wedding, and getting settled here. Now, why don't you go get what you need, and I'll start taking the pieces out of the first box."

CHAPTER SIX

When Marty got to her car, she called Jeff who promptly answered, "Good morning, Mrs. Combs. Have I told you I love you today?"

Marty laughed and answered, "I believe those were the first words out of your mouth quite early this morning, but I'm not complaining."

"How's the appraisal going?" he asked.

"I haven't started on the actual items, but the preliminary walk-through has been extraordinary. Their home and the grounds are beautiful, and they seem to be very nice people. Actually, that's why I'm calling. We've been invited to attend the cocktail party at the Rutledge Polo Club that John and Max are catering tonight. If you're free, I'd really like to go. I know nothing about polo, and I may never have another chance like this one to learn something about the sport. Are you up for it?"

"Don't even need to hesitate on that one. I'd definitely like to do it. I've been to one polo match in my life, so that hardly qualifies me as an expert. Do you want to meet me at home or what?"

"Yes. Pia handed me an invitation, and the party starts at 6:30. I'll leave here about 5:00, so we can meet at home and then come together. I better get back in the house and start earning my keep. See you tonight. By the way, I love you too!"

Marty opened the trunk of her car and slung her camera bag over her shoulder. She took out her briefcase with its measuring tape and flashlight along with some soft cotton gloves and fabrics which she sometimes used when she was handling or photographing an art object.

When she got back to the sitting room, she took her camera from its case and mounted it on a tripod. She opened the shutters on the windows to allow maximum light to come into the room and then she turned to Pia, who was taking a vase out of the first box.

Marty stared at it and whispered, "Pia, do you know where your parents got that vase or anything about it?"

"No, as I said earlier, I know next to nothing about their collection. Why do you have that funny look on your face?"

"If that vase is what I think it is, it's worth hundreds of thousands of dollars. One just like it sold at auction several years ago. Only four were made, and the bidding was fierce for it. Do you know if your parents went to auctions or had people buy for them?"

"Again, I don't know anything about how they acquired their collection, but this vase is quite pretty with these two little winged figures on the side." She turned it over in her hands.

"Pia, set it down very gently on the rug, and I mean very gently." Marty carefully picked the vase up and looked at the bottom of it through a magnifying glass. "Look," she said excitedly, "there's the signature of Rene Lalique. I thought he was the artist who made the vase. I'm almost certain this is the vase that was sold at auction, and no wonder your parent's estate was small. This vase alone is worth over a quarter of a million dollars." She sat back to see what affect her words had on Pia.

"I can't believe it," Pia said with a look of astonishment on her face. "They never talked about what things were worth. Of course, for years we never talked, period. When we finally reconciled they were old and ill. Although they loved their collection, it probably wasn't a high priority for them in their last few years." She looked at her watch. "Marty, I really do need to do a few things to get ready for the cocktail party. If you need me for anything, just ask Lupe to get me. Please join Jack and me for lunch. You'll need to take some kind of a break and eat something. We'll have lunch in the kitchen, and the cook, Taffy, is quite good. See you later," she said as she stood up and walked out of the room.

Marty spent the next two hours taking glass pieces out of boxes, measuring them, photographing them, running her finger over them to detect flaws and chips, and generally being in an overall state of awe.

Any museum in the world would be thrilled to have just one of the pieces in this collection, much less the whole collection. It's got to be worth well over several million dollars, and to think Pia doesn't have a clue what it's worth. I can't imagine having it trucked out to Los Angeles in the back of a U-Haul truck.

There was a soft knock on the open door. Marty looked up and saw Lupe. "Excuse me, ma'am, but Mrs. Marshall asked me to tell you that lunch is being served."

"Thanks, Lupe, I'll be there shortly. I just need to take a couple more photos of this Tiffany lamp." She took photos from several angles and then walked out of the suite and down the hall to the kitchen where Pia and Jack were engrossed in a conversation. They were so absorbed in talking to each other they didn't see her come in.

"Pia, trust me on this," she overheard Jack saying. "The guy's a cheat. He gives polo a bad name. He's threatened me for years, because my team is the best in the United States and has won far more matches than his team. I can't tell you how many times he's tried to bribe my team members trying to get them to join his team. He even tried to bribe my vet to give my horses drugs to dope them, so they'd underperform when we were playing a match. I've given everyone who has anything to do with the polo club strict instructions that if he's seen near the barns or workout areas, they're to call the police and me immediately. Actually, I keep a couple of guns in the barns as well as in the house."

Pia started to say something when Jack looked up, sensing that Marty had entered the room. "I was just having a conversation with Pia regarding an unethical polo person. I guess it doesn't matter what the profession or the game is, there will always be someone who has a crooked agenda," he said as he passed a platter of chicken breasts in a sauce to Marty.

"This looks wonderful! What is it?"

Taffy was washing dishes. She looked over at Marty and said, "It's chicken cordon bleu, or as some people would call it, chicken stuffed with ham and cheese. I like to serve it with a raspberry chipotle sauce."

Marty cut a piece of her chicken and ate it. "Taffy, this is incredible. My compliments to the chef."

A moment later Jack asked, "So what do you think of Pia's art glass collection?"

"It's the best I've ever seen, hands down. I'm sorry to do this, but the value of it will be well into the millions. The reason I'm sorry is this means you'll have to pay the insurance premiums on it, and that won't be cheap."

"Well, I'm lucky. The high tech companies were very good to me, so money isn't a problem. What is a problem is making sure Kevin Sanders stays as far away from here as possible. That's what the problem is."

Pia put her hand on his arm and said, "Jack, let it go. With the security you have around the house, the barns, and the polo club, I don't think that will be a problem, but I am curious how he got past the security shack today."

"When I kicked him out, I called security and asked that very question. Evidently Kevin told the guard he had an appointment to see me regarding a horse I wanted to sell him. As if I'd let him near one of my horses."

"Jack, I asked Marty if she and her husband could join us for the cocktail party tonight. It turns out a friend of hers is catering it."

"I don't know a thing about it. Nicky, my administrative assistant is in charge of it." He turned to Marty and asked, "Who's your friend?"

"He's the owner of The Red Pony food truck. He started a catering business a few months ago, because the Pony had become so popular and people were asking him to cater events for them. He even had to get a second truck. He's developed quite a business, and I think you'll be very happy with Nicky's selection of him. By the way, I called my husband, and we'd love to attend the party. Thanks for the invitation. Neither one of us knows much about polo, so we're really looking forward to it."

"Well, if you don't mind, let me take a couple of minutes to tell you about the sport of polo," Jack said. "After all, next to my love for Pia, my bride-to-be, it's my other great love.

"The history of the sport goes back thousands of years to when mounted nomads in Central Asia played a version of polo. The game followed the nomad migration to Persia where it was known to be played sometime between 600 B.C. and 100 A.D. The modern version of polo originated in India, where in 1859 the Silchar Polo Club was founded by some British military officers. The game spread to England and soon to the United States, where the first game was played in New York in 1876.

"As you no doubt know, polo is a team sport played on horseback. There are four players on each team. The objective is to score goals against an opposing team. Players score by hitting a small ball with a wooden mallet and driving the ball into the opponent's goal. Since the players are mounted on full size horses racing at breakneck speeds, they need a lot of field area for the horses to negotiate. The typical grass polo field is three hundred yards long and one hundred sixty yards wide. The modern polo game lasts approximately two hours and is divided into periods called chukkas.

"You've probably heard the term 'polo pony,' but that's an historical phrase from years ago when the polo horses were much smaller. Today's modern polo ponies are full size horses bred for maximum speed, stamina, and agility.

"Today there are more than two hundred seventy-five polo clubs registered in the United States and the United States Polo Association has more than 4,500 members.

"So, enough about polo, let's get back to tonight's party. I have this cocktail party annually," Jack said. "People fly in from all over for it. I think a couple of people from Argentina will even be here tonight. I introduce this year's team, and I have the horses walked around the polo grounds in their full colors. What I'm trying to do is get everyone excited for the upcoming season, and I've found if I do it earlier than everyone else, I'm ahead of the game. My team loves it, because they can kind of bask in the glory for the next few months, but it also serves to let everyone know that our team is very, very serious about polo, and we intend to again be the number one team in the United States and quite possibly the world."

*****

Kevin Sanders strode to his car, red-faced, furious, and knowing his elevated blood pressure wasn't good for a man his age with a family history of hypertension.

How dare Jack tell me not to set foot on his property. Who does this relatively new kid on the polo block think he is? Comes in with all that money he got in high techs from Northern California and becomes an instant authority on the game. Right. While he was making his billions, I was traveling around the world with a polo mallet in my hand. I know the guys on his team, and the only reason they stay is for the money. He pays his team more than any of the other owners, which makes us all look bad. Before he came to town I was number one, and I intend to do everything in my power to become number one again.

Kevin looked at the people setting up for the event that was going to be held on the Rutledge Polo Club grounds that evening. Everywhere he looked workers were edging, mowing grass, taking tables and chairs from party rental trucks, and in general scurrying to get everything done before the guests started to arrive.

Sure glad that Lex, my doctor, told me he had to go out of town today and asked if I needed an extra ticket for tonight. He doesn't know anything about the bad blood between Jack and me. I told him I had a friend who would love to come. I think I've come up with a way to ruin Jack's wonderful new life. I want him to feel the pain of what it's like to have your world fall out from under you, and I know my plan is a good one. Yeah, Jack, get ready for your big night, because this is one you'll probably never forget.

He drove down the lane to the guard shack and waved at the guard. *Hope the guards are ready for a big surprise tonight,* he thought as he smiled thinking about what the evening would bring for Jack.

CHAPTER SEVEN

Gerta Martelli, a dowdy looking middle-aged woman with mousy brown hair interspersed with grey, walked off the plane and into the Palm Springs airport and thought, *so this is what Palm Springs is like. From their suntans, it looks like all anyone does here is play golf or tennis or sunbathe. I can see why people want to live here in the winter, but I don't think I'm going to like the heat. From what the weather channel said, it's going to be 102 degrees today, and that is not my idea of fun. I sure didn't expect it to be this hot.*

Tired from a long travel day that included two airport layovers in order to get to Palm Springs, she walked over to the rental car counter. A little later she and her luggage were in a rental car. The clerk had given her a city map and circled the hotel where she'd made her reservation as well as the location of the Rutledge Polo Club. The clerk had looked at her curiously and asked Gerta if she was aware that the polo season didn't start until January which was several months away. Gerta had been noncommittal in her answer as she walked away from the booth.

She'd struggled with what she should do about her parents' art glass collection ever since her parents had died and left it to Pia. She still couldn't believe that after she'd spent the last few years living with her parents and taking them to their various doctors, making meals for them, arranging for someone to clean their house, and everything else she'd done, her parents had willed the art glass collection and their house to Pia. Gerta was well aware of what the collection was worth and knew it was far more valuable than the proceeds from the sale of the house Pia had given to her.

She got mad all over again every time she thought about how sanctimonious Pia had been when she'd told Gerta she felt the only fair thing to do was for one of them to take the house and the other one to have the collection, rather than Pia having both of them. What particularly irked Gerta was that she knew Pia didn't have a clue what the collection was worth and could just as easily have given it to Gerta, and Pia could have taken the proceeds from the sale of the house.

Gerta knew Pia's life hadn't been easy, and as much as it galled her, she'd decided to just let it go and get on with her own life. She figured that was probably why her parents had willed the house and the collection to Pia. After all of the years of being a spinster and taking care of her parents, Gerta had finally met a man she was very interested in and who'd made several comments that led her to believe he was going to ask her to marry him. Given that development in her life, she'd decided to let the past go - until a few days ago.

She and Pia were never the type of sisters who called each other on the phone several times a week and shared what was going on in their lives. At the most they talked about once every two or three months, so when Pia called to tell Gerta she was moving to Palm Springs from Los Angeles in two days and would soon be getting married, she was shocked. Pia told her she'd never been happier and that her husband-to-be was very wealthy and owned the Rutledge Polo Club in Palm Springs. She said he owned a large mansion, and she was going to have her own suite of rooms. She'd asked Gerta to come to the wedding. Gerta had told her she needed to check her schedule at the school where she was a teacher and see if she could get the time off.

Gerta had been in shock just thinking about what Pia had told her. It didn't seem fair that Pia had not only gotten the valuable art glass collection, but now she'd also be marrying a man who seemed to be really, really, wealthy. It just wasn't right.

She decided the only thing she could do was fly to Palm Springs and talk to Pia. Gerta would have to make Pia understand that the collection should go to Gerta now that Pia was going to be marrying such a wealthy man. It was early evening when she got to her hotel, and she was exhausted from the long day of travel as well as the time change, but even so, she needed to call Pia.

She punched in Pia's number and heard her voice say, "Hello, Gerta, is that you?"

"It is, and I have a surprise for you. My school's on a break, so I decided to fly to Palm Springs and see you and meet your husband-to-be. I'm at the hotel now. I also want to talk to you about Mom and Dad's art glass collection which you'll probably want to give me now that you're going to be marrying into wealth."

"Well, that's great, but your timing is a little off. Tonight we're having dinner with Jack's polo team, and tomorrow is completely filled with appointments. Jack's having a large cocktail party at the Rutledge Polo Club tomorrow evening. Why don't you come to it? I'll call security and tell them to let you in. Would that work for you?"

"Yes, I can be there, but I really do think it's only fair that you give me the collection."

Pia was quiet for a long moment, and then she said, "Gerta, Mom and Dad willed the house to me as well as the collection. That was their wish. I gave you the proceeds from the house. No, I won't be parting with the collection. It's mine, and if something happens to me it will go to Jack. We've decided we're kind of old fashioned about what's his is mine and vice-versa. I've got to go. Jack's motioning for me to end the call, or we're going to be late to dinner. The party starts at 6:30 tomorrow night. I'm looking forward to seeing you and having you meet Jack. The people at the security shack will be expecting you and will let you in. I'll text you with the address." With that she ended the call.

Gerta looked at her phone in fury and disbelief. *Pia couldn't even make time tomorrow to see her one and only sister? And what's up with that "What's his is mine, and what's mine is his?" Sounds like she's going to will the collection to him, and I'll be left completely out in the cold. Think there's some saying about the rich get richer and the poor get poorer. I remember in some class in college we studied Karl Marx talking about economic inequality. It didn't mean much to me then, but if this isn't the perfect example of it, I don't know what is.*

A dark thought arose in her mind and she immediately squelched it, but it kept coming back. She went down to the hotel coffee shop and had a hamburger with fries. Tonight was a night when she needed some comfort food, because her world had been turned upside down. Try as she might to stop thinking about it, the dark thought she had earlier kept coming back, the thought that if Pia died before she got married and signed a will or a trust, the collection would rightfully, under the law, go to her as Pia's closest relative.

She felt exhausted when she returned to her room, and soon she fell into bed and slept fitfully through the night. When she awoke in the morning the only thing she could think about was that in just a few short weeks she would forever lose her claim to the art glass collection. If something happened to Pia once she was married, it would go to her husband, Jack Rutledge. The thought came to her that she had to do something to prevent that from happening, and if it meant something bad had to happen to Pia, so be it. They weren't close, and her parents were dead. She knew her parents wouldn't want the collection they'd spent a lifetime assembling, not to mention the joy and pride they'd had in it, to go to a man they'd never met. She walked over to the desk in the hotel room and booted up her laptop. Within minutes she found what she was looking for and knew how she would be spending a good part of her day.

A sad crooked smile crossed her face as she thought about the events that would be taking place, but she knew she had no other choice. Resolutely, she walked down the hall to the elevator, ready for breakfast, knowing she had to be strong for what was going to take place that evening.

CHAPTER EIGHT

Roberto picked up his phone and said, "Battisto here. Is that you, Dominic?"

"Yeah, just checkin' in with my favorite restaurateur and nephew. Your numbers from last month look pretty good, Berto. Looks like this year's gonna' be better than last year. Wonder if yer' up to openin' another restaurant. Sal called a little while ago and said I need to find somewhere to dump some money. Lookin' fer a place that won't set off all the bells and whistles at the IRS or FBI. I was thinkin' a restaurant might be a good place. Thinkin' of an upscale one down in Orange County, say in Laguna Beach or Newport Beach. Plenty of money down there, and people always love a classy high end Italian joint. Whaddya think?"

"Yeah, I'm up for it. Last time I was down in Laguna Beach, I saw a lot of Frenchy and high-end restaurants, and even had the thought Laguna could sure use an upscale Italian one. With the Pageant of the Masters and the Sawdust Festival, summertime's a zoo down there, and people are always lookin' for somewhere to go for dinner before the Pageant or after they've been to the Festival. In the winter months they get a lot of European visitors because of their location and it being an artsy town. Want me to check out the real estate and see what's available?"

"Get on it. Sooner we get started the sooner I can get Sal off my back. So, how ya' doin'? Sal told me he'd heard from a little birdie that the Italian looker ya' was seein' left ya' fer some polo guy that she's gonna' marry. I tol' him the birdie must be wrong, because being' Rocco's son, you'd never let some broad leave ya'. Also told him I wasn't leavin' my part of the Family business to some wuss who'd let a woman get away from him, least not if he wanted her, and from what I heard, ya' wanted her."

Roberto was quiet for a few moments trying to figure out what he should say to save face. Finally, he answered Dominic. "Yeah," he said laughing, "the broad decided she liked horses more than she liked Italian food. Her loss."

Now it was Dominic's turn to be quiet. In a voice that held menacing undertones he said, "Might wanna rethink lettin' the broad leave ya', Berto. Don't make ya' look too good, and if the rest of the Family hears about it, don't think they'd want a man runnin' the Family business when he can't even keep the woman he wanted. No, Berto, make the problem go away, or I will. Can't have my nephew lookin' like a fool. I promised your dad, Rocco, I'd look out fer ya' when he was gone. Well, he's gone, but if yer' gonna' make a fool of yerself, I can't help ya'. Like I said, make the problem go away."

While his cell phone was still pressed against his ear, Roberto felt sweat trickling down the back of his neck. He stood up and began to pace the room, pausing to look in a large mirror. The man who looked back at him appeared to be a very successful Italian businessman who obviously spared no expense on his physical appearance, from his private trainer-toned body, to his carefully trimmed salt and pepper haircut. His designer clothes fit so well it was obvious they'd been tailored just for him. That man feared no one, particularly not a small dark-haired middle-aged Italian woman.

He smiled at the reflection of the large diamond pinkie ring he wore, the ring his father had given him on his deathbed. He'd made a promise to Rocco that he would never do anything to cause the Family shame, and that he would follow in Rocco's footsteps. He knew what he had to do for his father and the Family.

"Dominic, it was a momentary lapse on my part. I'll have someone take care of the matter within a couple of days. By this time next week, it will be old news. Trust me, this will never happen again. Anyway, she'd used up her usefulness to me. I'll call you after the matter has been taken care of."

"I'll be waitin' for yer' call, Berto. See that ya' don't disappoint me or the Family. By the way, the little birdie who tol' Sal about yer' little problem also tol' me that the man she's gonna marry is havin' a big cocktail party next week at the polo club he owns in Palm Springs. Thought maybe ya' could call and express some interest in bein' an investor in his team. Might get ya' or whoever's gonna take care of this problem into the party. Talk to ya' later." Dominic didn't wait for a response from Roberto and ended the call.

Roberto went back to his desk, dreading the upcoming telephone call he knew he had to make. There was no other way to handle the problem his uncle had called him about. He'd made a deathbed promise to his father and that was that. The Family was more important than anything else. Even though he knew Dominic regarded him as the son he'd never had, if this problem wasn't taken care of, Dominic would make certain that Roberto was taken care of. Some things were inviolate, and this was one of them. The man who had been tapped to lead the Family could never be seen as weak, particularly when it came to a woman.

He pressed Luigi's telephone number into his cell phone and immediately heard his voice saying, "Hey, Boss, got somethin' fer me?"

"Yes, there's a little matter I need taken care of. Her name is Pia Marshall. I'm sending you a photo of her as we speak. She's moving to Palm Springs in a few days and is going to marry the man who owns the Rutledge Polo Club, a privately owned polo club there. I hear he's very wealthy, and he's hosting a cocktail party at the polo club next week. I'm going to call the polo club and express interest in investing in the team, but I'll tell whoever I talk to that first I'd like for my assistant to see the grounds, the training facilities, and the barns, plus I'd like him to attend the party. I assume they've issued invites or tickets to get onto the grounds. I Googled the polo club, and it's got a security shack. As soon as I get the invite or ticket, I'll have it couriered to you. That will get you in. I'll call to let you know when to expect it. Think you can handle this?"

"Not a problem. Not the first time I've had to handle somethin' like this for ya'. Nothin' will ever link me to her death."

"It better not," Roberto said. "One more thing, I know sometimes you play rough. I want this to be over with fast with as little pain as possible to her. Got it?"

"Got it, Boss. I'll wait for yer' call."

Roberto pressed the red button on his phone and ended the call as a feeling of nausea washed over him. The perks to being the number two man in the West Coast Family were huge, but sometimes, like now, he momentarily wondered what his life would have been like if he hadn't been born into the Family. It was a fleeting thought, one that was usually eased by two fingers of Maker's Mark straight up. He walked over to the bar, poured the drink, and quickly knocked it back, waiting for the warmth from the whiskey to get rid of the numbing cold he felt. This time it took awhile.

*****

After Roberto's call, Luigi stood by the window in his home office, thinking what would be the best way to kill Pia Marshall. In the past work he'd done for Roberto, he'd always used the Mafia's preferred method of a close range shot to the temple from a .22 pistol. Since Roberto wanted it to be quick and from the way he'd talked, probably not leave any bloody mess, Luigi knew he was going to have to be a little creative.

While he stood there he remembered a recent conversation he'd had with one of the other members of the Family, Nuccio. He'd told Luigi that his boss, Mario, had him take out Mario's wife. The Family didn't like attention drawn to it through divorces. Evidently Mario's wife had seen a lawyer and was going to file for divorce, because she'd found out about Mario's long-time mistress and that he was the father of her child. Mario had told Nuccio to get rid of her, but he didn't want a mess or for her to suffer, since he didn't want his children hurt any more than necessary by her death.

Nuccio told Luigi he'd used chloroform which was easy to buy, and it caused instant death when used in excess of the recommended amounts. Luigi scrolled through web sites on his phone and found several places that sold chloroform over the counter to be used as a solvent. As luck would have it, a large hardware store that stocked industrial solvents and cleaners happened to be very close to his home. He called the store, and the young woman who answered the phone assured him they had plenty of chloroform in stock. He made a mental note to buy it and some heavy duty medical gauze pads on his way out of town when he went to Palm Springs. He smiled, thinking how happy Roberto was going to be when he found out that Luigi had been able to make his problem go away.

CHAPTER NINE

Marty spent the afternoon appraising one art glass piece after another. The collection was so spectacular she felt like she was the only one who held the key to a museum. She'd appraised other art glass collections with far more pieces in them, but quality-wise, this was the best she'd ever seen, and to think it was in a private collection. She felt humbled she'd actually been able to hold the pieces in her hands.

The floor of Pia's bedroom was covered with the pieces Marty had taken out of the boxes. She had no idea where Jack and Pia planned to put the collection, but hoped it would be in a special location that was relatively earthquake proof. The thought of one of the pieces tumbling to the tile floor in an all too common Southern California trembler was one she didn't want to dwell on.

She made a mental note to remind them to secure the pieces with a sticky putty like substance that had been developed just for that very purpose. All of the museums used it. She assumed Jack probably had his art pottery pieces secured with it since they were highly breakable, but she wanted to make sure the glass pieces were also properly secured and as safe from harm as possible.

When she'd finished measuring, inspecting, and photographing the art glass, she walked down the hall and heard voices coming from the library. Pia and Jack were sitting side by side on a brown suede couch looking over what appeared to be a list. She knocked on the open door to announce herself.

"Come in, Marty," Pia said. "We were just going over the guest list for tonight, and like I told you earlier, other than my sister who's visiting here in Palm Springs, and Jack's son, I don't know anyone who's coming to the party. I'm so glad you'll be there, so at least I'll have someone to talk to," Pia said laughing.

"Pia, trust me," Jack said, "as my wife-to-be there will be a line of people wanting to talk to you. Everyone's curious about the woman I'm going to marry. If anything, you'll be so tired from talking and meeting people, that the only thing you're going to want to do when this is over is go to sleep for a very long time."

Later, Marty would remember Jack's words and wonder if he had some sort of an inner sense about what would take place that night.

"You can count on me being next to you tonight, Pia," Marty said. "Don't worry. I'm sure everyone will think Jack made a very wise decision when he decided to marry you. To change the subject, I'm finished with the art glass collection. Jack, do you want me back here tomorrow to do your art pottery collection, or do you want to wait a couple of days, so you two can recuperate from the party?"

"I'd like you to come back tomorrow. The sooner I can get these things insured, the better I'll feel. What did you think about Pia's collection?" he asked.

"Quite simply, it's the best I've ever seen, in or out of a museum. It's priceless. I'm afraid the insurance premium on it will be hefty, but as priceless as those pieces are, they definitely need to be insured."

"Really?" Pia asked. "As I told you earlier, I know nothing about art glass, and I certainly never thought the collection was as good as you're saying it is. I'm glad I didn't know that when I packed up the pieces and drove them out to California from New Jersey. I think I even left the door of the U-Haul truck unlocked when I stayed in a couple of motels. It's probably just as well I didn't know the value of the collection. I would have been a nervous wreck."

"Jack," Marty said, "it would make me feel a lot better if you called Dick at the insurance company and asked him if you can get some temporary insurance, it's called a binder, to insure the pieces for three million dollars as of today. Tell him I'll get the appraisal to him within a week. I'll make it a priority. I really don't like to think you're having a big affair on the grounds here tonight, and a collection worth that much is in the house and uninsured. I'm sure none of your guests would enter the house, and I'm guessing since neither of you knew the value of the collection or what was actually in it, you haven't told anyone about it. It's just so incredibly good I really want to see an insurance binder put on it."

"Sure, if you think it's that important, I'll do it right now." He stood up and walked over to the house phone on his desk and placed a call to Dick at the insurance company. When he finished the call he turned to Marty and said, "There, it's done. The binder will be in effect momentarily."

"Pia, I've got to be leaving now," Marty said. "I'll see you in a little while, and thanks again for the invitation. Polo is a whole new world to me."

"Well, consider yourself in good company. It's a whole new world for me as well. See you later."

*****

Marty and Jeff arrived at the compound where they lived at almost the same moment. They opened their car doors and hurried to each other, both of them eager for a hug and a kiss from their new spouse. Jeff was the first to pull away, and when he did he held Marty at arms' length, looking at her with a broad smile on his face.

"Marty, don't want the chief to know this, but all I could think about at work today was that I had to be the luckiest man in the world to be married to you. Thank you for agreeing to be my wife."

"At the risk of sounding schmaltzy, I'll echo that sentiment, and if you look over at the gate, I think you'll see that Duke's beginning to

39

realize this is a permanent situation. Judging by how fast his tail is wagging, I think he's just fine with it."

They both looked over at the big black Labrador retriever who looked like he was grinning. He was in his customary position, waiting at the gate, which he did whenever Marty was away from the compound. Much to Jeff's chagrin, and somewhat to Marty's, he refused to walk on the desert floor. No amount of threats or coaxing had worked. Marty had done some research on her computer and came across an ad for dog booties. She'd decided to see if that would work out in the desert. He was a little big to carry out there every time he needed to commune with nature. Although she wasn't thrilled about it now, whenever she walked him past the gate to take care of business, on went the pink booties.

"Jeff, I'll take Duke out for a walk and feed him while you start to get dressed. I won't be long. I think you're really going to enjoy tonight. Back in a minute."

She took the booties from the pouch she'd attached to the side of the wooden gate and slipped them on Duke. A few minutes later they returned to the compound, and she fed him his dinner.

Marty hurriedly dressed and noticed Jeff was putting his police service pistol in the holster attached to his belt. "Jeff, do you really have to bring that with you tonight? I mean, this is a party at the polo club. Why would you possibly need it there?"

"Sorry, Sweetheart, but you better get used to it. I've been called out of parties and all sorts of events when something bad goes down, and I've found if I have my gun with me it sure saves me from going home or to the station to get it. Don't worry. I'll wear a blue sport coat over it, and no one will ever know I even have it on me.

"As you can see, I listened when you told me on the phone what the color scheme for tonight was going to be. I'm appropriately dressed in white pants, a red and white striped shirt, and a blue blazer. I should fit right in, and I have to say you look fabulous. I think the blue and white hat adds a nice touch to your outfit. Ready?"

*****

"I know where the Rutledge Polo Club's located. I'm assuming we're going there. Right?" Jeff said as he began the thirty-minute drive towards Palm Springs from the high desert area where their compound was located.

"Yes. Pia said she'd leave my name at the gate, so we could get in. She's pretty nervous about this whole thing. That's why she asked me to come. She told me that other than her sister and Jack's son, she won't know anyone who will be attending."

"Having lived in Palm Springs for a number of years and being a police detective, I imagine I'll know a few of the people there. By the way, I forgot to ask you how the appraisal went today. Did you see some good stuff?"

"No," Marty answered. "I didn't see some good stuff. What I saw was simply the best art glass that could be assembled in a collection in or out of a museum. I mean when you have pieces by Lalique, Daum, Tiffany, and a bunch of the other fine French and American art glass makers, it makes a collection priceless. I asked Jack, he's the owner of the polo club and the man Pia's going to marry, to call Laura's boss, Dick, and request an insurance binder of three million dollars. I don't think I'd be able to sleep tonight knowing the collection was uninsured."

"Seriously, Marty? Three million dollars for glass? Sure sounds like an awful lot of money."

"Yes, Jeff, seriously. It could even be worth more than that. I'll know more in a couple of days. This has to go to the top of my to-do list although in a case like this it's hard to put prices on items that are so rare I know I'm going to have problems coming up with comparables."

Jeff turned and looked at her as he pulled off the freeway and said, "That's an interesting situation. What do you do when you can't find a comparable price for an object you have to appraise?"

She paused for a moment before she spoke and then said, "It's going to sound rather self-serving and egotistic, but that's where my experience comes in. If what I've seen is incomparable, and I have to evaluate it anyway, I'll put a value on it that I think is fair for the quality, the beauty, the rarity, and the demand for the item. When it's that rare you can bet there would be a huge demand for it if it did go to auction or was put up for sale. Every collector who has the funds to buy the piece will want it, and it would result in a huge bidding war which would further drive up the value. Bottom line, it's a judgment call on my part, and I guess the good news is, when there's nothing comparable, who can say that my judgment isn't right?"

"I don't know. I tend to be a more logical person and that sounds pretty pie in the sky to me," Jeff said.

"You're absolutely right, and that's why being an appraiser appealed to me. I always hated logic and math, and I think a lot better out of the box. This is one of the few professions that lets me do it. Oh, we're here. Turn down this lane. The house is at the far end of it, but we need to go to the polo club grounds on the left. The guard shack is just up ahead."

"Wow, Marty, the house is incredible. It's one of the most beautiful I've ever seen and perfect for the desert. Nice cushy job you have unlike some of us who have to chase and catch bad guys."

"Uh-huh. Just be on your best behavior tonight, because I intend to charge a nice fat fee for expediting this appraisal."

Jeff always drove his police issued car since he never knew when he'd have to leave when a crime had taken place and a detective was needed. Tonight was no exception, but he wouldn't need his police car because the crime that would be taking place was at the Rutledge Polo Club.

CHAPTER TEN

"Marty, can I get you something to drink? Since I'm on call tonight, I'll be drinking club soda. I also want to say hi to John and Max if I can find them," Jeff said.

"Yes, I'd love a glass of white wine. Whatever they have is fine. I'm going to find Pia and see how she's doing. Oh, there she is," Marty said. "You can't miss a woman that beautiful with jet black hair. When you bring the wine to me just look for the hair. It's kind of like a beacon in the night." She walked over to where Pia was deep in conversation with a woman.

Marty tapped her on the shoulder. "Hi, Pia. I just wanted to let you know I'm here, but I don't want to interrupt your conversation. I can come back later."

"No, that won't be necessary," Pia said. "I'd like you to meet my sister. Gerta, this is Marty, the appraiser I told you about. We're just discussing the art glass collection our parents willed to me. My sister thinks since I'm getting married to a wealthy man, I should give it to her. I told her I wasn't going to do that."

"It's nice to meet you, Gerta. I hope you're enjoying your visit to Palm Springs."

"No, as a matter of fact I'm not. I really thought Pia would be a little more reasonable about the collection, but I guess there's not much I can do to convince her it should be mine. After all, it seems pretty unfair for one person to get everything, doesn't it?" she asked. "So what do you think the collection is worth? I guess it really doesn't matter, since it looks like I'm not going to get it, but just for the record I'd like to know what I'm not getting." She turned and looked at Pia with a look of pure hatred.

Marty saw nothing but sorrow in Pia's eyes. It was clear to Marty that the preceding conversation with her sister had been very painful for Pia. She turned to Gerta and said, "I'm sorry, but it would be unethical for me to answer your question. If Pia chooses to discuss it with you, that's up to her, but I can't."

"Fine. So long, Pia. I'm out of here and out of your life. At some point, I hope you find out that money can't keep you safe or make you happy," Gerta said as she stormed towards the door, muttering to herself.

"Well, I guess that's one less person who will be coming to the wedding," Pia said with a dismayed look on her face. "As I mentioned to you this morning, my parents willed their house and their art glass collection to me, not Gerta. I thought it was pretty generous of me to give her the proceeds from the house, but it looks like she doesn't agree with me."

"Pia, the one thing I've learned since I've been appraising is that if there's money attached to an object, someone in the family is going to want it. I've seen old pottery pieces that were used to hold pencils, and when I told the person it was quite rare and valuable, it suddenly became very important to them.

"Conversely, I've seen objects that have been handed down from generation to generation with the admonishment that it was quite valuable so be careful with it. When I told them it was actually quite a common item and worth very little, it lost all its appeal for them. I find it interesting how many people define themselves by their stuff."

"Well, I'm sorry you had to witness such an unpleasant scene between two sisters. It was inexcusable behavior on Gerta's part. So now one of the two people I knew on the party list is not speaking to me. There's the other one on the list, Jack's son," Pia said motioning towards a group of men standing nearby. "I'd like you to meet him." She indicated Marty was to follow her over to where a handsome man in his late thirties was standing talking to several people. The resemblance to Jack was amazing. He was simply a younger version.

Jensen saw his stepmother-to-be walking up to the group and excused himself. "Hi, Pia. I think the party's going great, don't you?" he asked.

"It seems to be, but since this is my first party at a polo club, I really have nothing to compare it to. Jensen, I'd like you to meet Marty Combs. She's doing an appraisal for your father and me."

He extended his hand and said, "Welcome to the Rutledge Polo Club. So what are you appraising for Dad and Pia?"

Pia answered for her. "Marty is quite ethical and won't discuss her appraisals, but I can, since what she's been appraising is mine. She's doing Jack's art pottery and the art glass collection that I inherited from my parents. Since Jack and I just signed a trust giving each other everything we own in case something happens to one of us, we thought we better find out what our collections are worth and get them insured."

Marty noticed the rapid expressions taking place on Jensen's face. First she saw shock and astonishment, and then she noticed a look of pure hatred flit across his face. The expression on his face smoothed out to one of neutrality, and he said, "I'm sorry Pia, but I don't understand what you mean."

"It's very simple, Jensen. I thought Jack told you we decided to sign the trust we had drawn up now rather than wait and have one more thing to do after we got married. I'm sorry you didn't know. I really thought you did."

"No, I didn't know, but I think it's wonderful both of you are so sure about the other one that you're leaving your respective estates to each other. I must admit I'm kind of surprised, because Dad's always told me that since I'm his only child his art pottery collection would go to me."

"Jensen, you know how busy he is getting ready for the polo

season and adding a wedding to the mix makes him even busier. I'm sure it just slipped his mind, and that's why he didn't tell you."

Just then Jeff walked up to them and Marty introduced Jensen and Pia to him. Jensen shook Jeff's hand and said, "If you'll excuse me, I need to talk to a couple of the team members. It was nice to meet both of you, and I hope we'll see you during the season."

"Great. Now I'm two for two," Pia said. "Let's go find Jack. Jeff, I'd like you to meet him." She turned around and started to walk over to where a crowd of people was gathered around Jack at the end of the barn. Marty mouthed the words, "I'll tell you later," to Jeff and followed her.

"There you are," Jack said in his customary booming voice. "Everyone, I want you to meet my bride-to-be, Pia Marshall. Please give her a round of applause for agreeing to marry this old man." Everyone in the group clapped and cheered.

Pia blushed and said, "Thank you. I want to get to know all of you, and I hope you'll be coming back here often." The crowd surrounding Jack began to break away until only the four of them were left. "Jack, I'd like you to meet my husband, Jeff Combs," Marty said. "You may have met before. Jeff's lived in the Springs for a long time, and he's a detective with the Palm Springs Police Department."

"Can't say that I have, Marty, but that's probably a good thing. Fortunately, I haven't needed the services of a detective, but if I ever do, at least now I know one," he said laughing.

Jack's cell phone rang and he said, "Excuse me. I need to take this call." He stepped away from them and listened. As he listened an angry look spread across his face. Pia made small talk with Marty and Jeff and looked over at Jack several times, clearly concerned. After a few minutes she excused herself and walked over to where he was standing. She put her hand on his arm as he ended the call.

"What's wrong, Jack? Your face is really red, and there's a vein on your neck that's pulsing."

"Remember when I told you at lunch about that scumbag, Kevin Sanders? That was the security guard at the security shack. The guard recalled seeing him when he was here earlier in the day and called to tell me he could be wrong, but he admitted a man about an hour ago who looked like him, although his invitation had a different name on it. The guard felt something was off, but he couldn't figure out what it was. He finally remembered and thought I should know."

"Has anyone seen him?" Pia asked. "I thought all of your security guards were going to be on the lookout for him."

"No, none of them has said anything. If that scumbag dares to come here tonight, I'll make such a public spectacle about it he'll wish he'd never darkened these grounds," Jack said making a fist with one hand and pounding the palm of his other hand with it.

"Oh, come on Jack, let it go. It's probably just a case of the guard being overly cautious since no one's seen him. Don't let that spoil the party for you."

"You're probably right, Pia. I just can't stand that guy. He's been a thorn in my side for years. Okay, it's behind me. I'm going to get something to drink."

Jeff and Marty couldn't help but overhear the conversation. "Marty, what's going on?" Jeff asked. She started to answer him, but stopped when Pia walked over to them.

"Why don't you go look at the horses?" Pia said. "They're really quite beautiful, and it's not often you can see that many good polo horses in one place, anyway that's what Jack tells me. I'm going outside for a moment. I've just about quit smoking entirely, but the last hour has been a little intense for me, and I think I can justify one. I'll meet you back here in the barn."

Marty and Jeff went from one stall to another talking to the groomers about the horses and learning what was involved in the sport of polo. "Jeff, I really would like to come to a couple of matches when the season starts. It sounds interesting."

"I agree. We'll definitely make that a priority after the first of the year. Oh, there's Jack."

Marty looked up and saw Jack walking towards them accompanied by a smaller older man with a neatly trimmed goatee that matched his perfectly combed shock of silver hair.

When Jack reached them he said, "Marty and Jeff, I'd like you to meet Dr. Rex Anderson. Although he's semi-retired, Rex has been my personal physician for years. In fact, Rex was one of the first people I met when I moved to Palm Springs. When he was younger, he was a terrific polo player, and today he's considered to be an expert on the history of the sport.

"Nice to meet you, Dr. Anderson," Jeff said as he and Marty shook hands with Dr. Anderson.

"Pleased to meet both of you, and call me Rex. What Jeff said about me is true. I'm semi-retired from practicing medicine, and I'm simply enjoying life after having worked as a doctor here in Palm Springs for over forty years. In fact, Jeff is one of only five or six patients I still see from time to time. So what brings the two of you to this little cocktail shindig Jack is throwing for all of us tonight?"

"I'm an art and antique appraiser doing some work for Jack and his bride-to-be, and my husband is a homicide detective with the Palm Springs Police Department," Marty said. "Jack and Pia were kind enough to invite us to tonight's party."

Turning to Jack, Marty said, "Jeff and I were just talking to your groomers and admiring your horses. They're absolutely beautiful."

"Thanks. My people do a very good job caring for the horses and training them, so they'll be ready for the polo matches. By the way, I can't seem to find Pia. Have you seen her?" he asked.

Marty glanced at her watch and said, "No. She said she needed a little break and suggested we look at some of the horses that are in their stalls, which we did. She said she'd meet us here in the barn, but that was almost an hour ago. I have no idea where she is."

Just at that moment Jensen ran up to where they were standing and breathlessly said to Jack, "Dad, quick. I need to talk to you. It's about Pia," he said grimly.

"What is it, Jensen?"

"You better come with me, Dad. I hate to tell you this, but two of the security guards saw a body lying on the ground behind the barn. They're not sure, but it might be Pia. They think she might be dead."

CHAPTER ELEVEN

Jack stared at Jensen in disbelief, as if he couldn't process what he'd just been told.

Jeff flashed his police badge at Jensen and said, "Jensen, take us to where she is. I'm a police detective, and I'd be the one called to investigate if there's any sign of foul play. Dr. Anderson, why don't you come with us in case there's an opportunity to provide lifesaving procedures to her?"

Jensen turned and quickly headed for the barn door followed by the other four. The movement brought Jack back from wherever he'd mentally retreated, and he shouted out in voice trembling with emotion, "Where is she, Jensen? Have you called an ambulance?"

"I'm sorry, Dad, but apparently there's no need for an ambulance," he said as he hurried towards the rear door of the barn. He opened the door and led them to where a group of guards were standing in a circle next to the back of the barn. In the center of the circle, lying face down on the ground, was the body of a woman with jet black hair. She wasn't moving and didn't appear to be breathing. It was Pia.

Dr. Anderson stepped forward and said in a strong tone of voice, "Everyone stand back. I'm a doctor, and I need to examine her."

When he gently rolled Pia's body over, there was a collective gasp from those watching him as they realized Pia's mouth and nose were tightly taped shut with grey duct tape. Some kind of a gauze bandage could be seen poking out from under the edges of the tape. Dr. Anderson quickly pulled the tape off of her face and carefully removed the gauze bandage covering her mouth and nose. A second gauze bandage had been wadded up and stuffed in her mouth. He removed the second bandage in order to clear her airway and see if she could breathe. He bent down and put his ear over her mouth, listening for any signs of breathing, but there were none.

Dr. Anderson looked up at Jack, his friend and patient of many years, and said in a somber voice, "Jack, I'm sorry, but she's gone. There's nothing I can do to save her."

He continued, "The gauze that was placed over her face and mouth is heavily saturated with chloroform. I recognize the sweet smell of it from when it was used in the medical profession years ago before the advent of newer and more modern anesthetics. It's a very strong anesthetic that can cause death if administered in too large of a dose. Evidently that's what happened to your poor Pia."

A guttural scream came from Jack as he knelt next to Pia's lifeless body and held her hand while tears welled up in his eyes. The people in the small group standing there seemed transfixed with the enormity of what they were looking at, and no one said a word.

Jeff broke the silence when, in a commanding voice, he spoke up and said to the security guards, "I'm a police officer. I want you to stand back and not come anywhere near here. This immediate area needs to be secured as a crime scene. Tell the guard at the guard shack not to let anyone leave the premises. I'm calling the station and reporting this as a homicide." Within moments sirens were heard in the distance as they approached the polo club.

In shock, Jack held Pia's hand in his, looked at the group standing slightly away from Pia's body, and in a tearful voice asked, "Who could do this? What did she ever do to anyone? Why, why her?"

"Jack, let's go to your house," Marty said. "There's nothing you can do right now by staying here. I'm so sorry. Jeff is very good at what he does, and he'll find out who did this. You don't need to stay here. I'll let Jeff know we're going to your house."

Jeff was busy telling several police officers that had arrived at the scene what he wanted done. Every person in attendance at the party was to be interrogated to see if they had seen or heard anything. With nearly one hundred guests at the party, it was going to be a long night for him and the other police officers.

"Jeff, I'm taking Jack to his house," Marty said. "He needs to grieve in private. I know you're going to probably be here most of the night. When you get through talking to John and Max, why don't you ask them to come to the house, and I can get a ride back to the compound with them."

"It's almost time for the party to end," Jeff said, "so I'll have someone interrogate them first. I'll see you at home later on. I also want you to remember to tell me what it was you were going to tell me. Right now, everything has relevance. Give me a couple of minutes, and I'll be up at the house to talk to Jack. You and Jack can leave now."

CHAPTER TWELVE

Marty and Jack walked over to his house. She asked him for his key and opened the door for them. Lupe was standing on the other side. "Mr. Rutledge, I heard police sirens. Is anything wrong?" she asked.

Jack walked past Lupe as if he never heard her and headed towards the library where he sat down heavily on a chair, his elbows on his knees, his hands holding his head. Lupe and Marty heard dry anguished sobs coming from him. Marty motioned for Lupe to follow her, and when they were out of Jack's earshot, she told Lupe what had happened.

"Oh no! I don't believe it. He's been so happy since he first met Miss Pia. Who would do something like that?" Lupe asked.

"I have no idea. My husband's a homicide police detective, and he's leading the investigation." Just then there was a knock on the door.

Lupe walked over to it and asked, "Who is it?"

"It's Detective Combs. I'm here with Jack's son."

"Lupe, where's Dad?" Jensen asked when she opened the door.

"He's in the library."

Jeff followed Jensen into the library, and Jensen walked over to where his father was sitting, staring off into space. "Dad, we'll find out who did this. I promise you," he said.

"Mr. Rutledge, I'm sorry to have to do this, but I need to ask you a few questions," Jeff said.

Jack turned towards Jeff, anguish written all over his face. "Yes, I'm sure you do have to ask me some questions. Let's get it over with. What do you want to know?"

"Did you or Pia have any enemies?"

Jack looked into space for a moment and then said, "Yes, I have a major enemy, someone who truly hates me. His name is Kevin Sanders, but he had nothing to do with Pia."

"Mr. Rutledge, motives can be very complicated. Perhaps he wanted to get back at you by killing Pia. Tell me everything you can about him."

Jack spent the next few minutes recounting his past with Kevin as well as his meeting with him earlier in the day. He went on to tell him about the call he'd gotten from the security guard at the gate.

"Do you know if he knew Pia?"

"No, but it wouldn't be too hard to find out what she looked like. Since I'm the owner of the polo club, there was a recent article in the Desert News about our upcoming marriage. Below it and off to the right was a picture of Pia and the comment that she was my beautiful Italian wife-to-be. She's pretty easy to spot with that jet black hair." He gulped and said in a ragged voice, "Was."

"Dad, I told the police who are working the crime scene at the barn that I'd be back in a few minutes. They want to interview me. I just wanted to check on you. I won't be long. I'll spend the night here." He turned to Lupe and said, "Would you call my house and have Jorge bring some clothes and toiletries over for me?"

"Of course, Mr. Rutledge."

"Marty, could you stay with Dad until I get back?"

"Certainly," she said as he walked out the door.

"Mr. Rutledge," Jeff continued, "I'll just be a few more minutes. Do you know if Pia had any enemies? Had she previously been married? What about children? Is there anything you can tell me about her that might be relevant?"

"We really didn't know each other all that well," Jack said. "We met at an antique show two months ago, and while I know that's not a very long time to know someone before you're going to get married, we didn't want to wait. I'll be sixty-two in a few weeks and at my age, who knows how much time you have left? All I know about Pia is that she was divorced and according to her, she'd made a big mistake when she married her husband. I know nothing more than that about him.

"We talked and decided we were going to spend the future together and we weren't going to dwell on the past. She did say she'd never had children, and that her parents were deceased. I know she has a sister. As a matter of fact, she was going to attend the cocktail party tonight, but I never had a chance to meet her."

"Mr. Rutledge, I understand Pia lived in Los Angeles prior to moving in here a few days ago. Was she employed while she lived in Los Angeles?"

"Yeah, seems kind of funny in a way. Rich old man falls for a shoe saleswoman. She was selling shoes when I met her. She worked until a few days ago, although I told her I'd like her to quit, and I'd support her until we got married, but she was kind of old-fashioned and didn't want to do that."

"Where did she work?"

"She sold shoes at Nordstrom's at their Westside Pavilion store.

She told me she couldn't afford to live near there, because the rents were so high, so she had quite a commute. Pia had a very small apartment. Working as a shoe saleswoman did not make her wealthy. I was really looking forward to sharing my wealth with her and treating her to things I know she'd never experienced, but now I never will," he said with a catch in his voice.

"I know how painful this must be, Mr. Rutledge, and truly I'm sorry to have to ask you these questions, but I'm almost through. Two things. First, I'd like a copy of the guest list, and I'd like to go over the names with you. Is there any way to check to see who actually came to the cocktail party that was on the guest list?"

"Yes," Jack said. "The security guards were to check off each person who was on the list when they arrived. They'd have a copy of it."

"All right. I'd like to see that checked list. Secondly, I understand you're divorced. How would you describe your relationship with your ex-wife?"

"We share a son, and I pay her alimony. That's about all I can say about Debbie. She had an affair, and when I found out about it I divorced her. I found out later that wasn't her first affair or probably her last. I pay her a lot of alimony every month, so she does her best not to make waves."

"Do you think she could have been jealous of Pia? Perhaps she didn't want to see you remarry. Is that a possibility?"

Jack was quiet for several long moments and then he said, "I really don't think so. She's a very gentle person. Debbie likes the good life, and my alimony allows her to lead that type of life. I honestly don't think she'd do anything to jeopardize it. No, I think pursuing her about Pia's death would be a dead end. She might not have been too thrilled that I was remarrying, but I really think that would be the extent of it."

There was a knock on the door, and Jensen walked in followed by

John and Max.

"Dad, I called Jorge and when he brings my things over, he's also going to bring some sleeping pills. I know you don't believe in them, but tonight's an exception. Please, you really should take one."

"Okay, you're probably right. I can't imagine going to sleep tonight."

"Jeff," John said, "You told me earlier you'd like us to take Marty home when we leave. The police have finished their interviews with Max and me, and we're getting ready to go home. Marty, can you come with us?"

Jeff spoke up. "Please take her home. Marty, I'm going to be here several more hours, and then I have to go to the station and write up a report. I don't think I'll be home until tomorrow morning. Get some sleep." He walked over to her and lightly kissed her.

Marty turned to where Jack was sitting and said, "Again, Jack, I am so sorry. Call me when you want me to appraise your art pottery collection. I'll write up the report of the art glass collection and get it to Dick within the week."

"Marty, actually I'd like you to appraise my art pottery collection tomorrow. It will take my mind off of this, or at least give me something else to think about. Can you come at ten tomorrow morning?"

"If you think you'll be up to it, I'll be happy to do it. You can tell me about some of the pieces, since I assume you researched them, and it will probably save me some time."

"Dad, don't you think that can wait a couple of weeks? You don't need anything else on your plate right now."

"No, Jensen. Since Pia and I were doing this together, I'd like to finish it as soon as possible. Otherwise, I'll keep thinking about her and her collection, although I guess it's mine now." He turned to

Marty and said, "I'll see you at ten tomorrow morning."

Jeff, John, Max, and Marty walked out of the house, three of them on their way home, while Jeff went back to where the other policemen were conducting interviews.

On the ride home they were very quiet. Murder has a way of stopping idle conversation.

CHAPTER THIRTEEN

When Marty, John, and Max got back to the compound, it was very dark, and it was clear Laura and Les had retired for the night. The only thing moving was Duke's tail at the gate, where he was patiently waiting for Marty, like he always did.

"See you in the morning, and thanks for the ride," Marty said.

"I need to get some sleep, Boss," Max said. "I'll be here tomorrow at the usual time." He walked over to where his car was parked, and John and Marty walked through the gate.

"Duke, might as well bootie you up. I need some sleep, and you need to take a walk. Let's go, big guy," she said as she pulled on his booties.

Sleep was slow in coming to Marty and finally at midnight she took two aspirin, wishing she had one of the sleeping pills Jensen had provided for Jack. Tonight was one of the few nights she felt she could justify one.

*****

The next morning Marty showered, dressed, walked Duke, and met the other residents of the compound in the courtyard for some coffee and sweet rolls John had laid out for them. A few minutes after she sat down Max came through the gate and walked into John's kitchen to start the prep work for the two food trucks, Max's and John's.

"Hear from John there was a little excitement at the polo club last night, and I see Jeff's car isn't here." Laura said. "Feel like talking about it?"

Marty spent the next half hour telling Laura and Les what had taken place the evening before. When she was finishing up, a very tired and haggard looking Jeff walked through the gate and sat down next to Marty.

"How about some coffee, Jeff? There's also some sweet rolls. I imagine you're ready to go to bed. Find out anything?" Marty asked.

"In answer to everything, no. I had so much coffee and so many sweet rolls last night, I'll probably never get some much needed sleep between my sugar and caffeine highs. As far as finding out anything, no, not a thing. It's a complete mystery, literally. By the way, I never had a chance to follow up with you last night when you said you'd tell me something later," he said looking at her. "Does it have anything to do with the murder?"

"I don't know, but I happened to be with Pia when she had a conversation with Jensen and then another one with her sister. Both conversations really upset Pia. I could see it on her face. The first was with her sister, Gerta." She told Jeff and the others about how angry Gerta had been regarding the art glass collection.

"Marty, would she have any way of knowing what it was worth?"

"I don't know. Pia mentioned that Gerta had taken care of her parents. Towards the end of their lives she'd moved in with them and been their caregiver. I would think she probably had some idea of the value of their collection, but I can't say for sure."

"What happened in the conversation with Jensen?" Jeff asked.

She told him Jensen had said he didn't know Pia and Jack had already signed a trust agreement so that their collections would go to each other, even though they weren't married.

"Wait a minute, Marty. Are you telling me Jensen thought he was going to inherit the collection and then he finds out his father has willed it to his bride-to-be?"

"Yes. That's what Pia told him, and he was clearly shocked by this revelation. He made the statement that Jack had told him as his only child he was going to inherit the collection."

Jeff was quiet for a few moments and then said, "Do you have any idea what Jack's collection is worth?"

"No. He had an appraisal done on it several years ago, and although I glanced at it yesterday, I never looked at the total amount. I will tell you he has a Rookwood lamp that's one of a kind and pretty priceless. If the rest of the collection is anywhere near that good, his collection will probably match or exceed hers in value."

"Think I need to take a closer look at Jensen. With Pia no longer in the picture, sonny boy will probably inherit everything when his father dies, and that's a powerful motive for murder."

Laura had been listening to the conversation and began to speak. "Jeff, I don't think it was Jensen. My intuition, or whatever you want to call it, doesn't see him as the murderer. Don't waste your time with him. Keep looking. I don't think Pia's murder had anything to do with Jack and his money, but I feel pretty certain it was someone Pia knew."

They all looked at Laura with respect. When Laura had been in college, she'd been part of a study testing people's abilities that went beyond the five senses. No one could explain what Laura sensed, but she'd been invaluable to Jeff in helping to solve the Meissen Monkey Band murder and another murder that had occurred at a local country music festival. She'd also helped with the murder that centered around an illegal collection of Native American artifacts. At first Jeff hadn't believed in her psychic abilities, but now when she spoke he listened.

"Are you getting anything else, Laura? Believe me, I can use all the help you can give me on this one."

"Wish I could, Jeff. I'm not getting anything about who did it, only who didn't do it, and that would be Jensen."

"Well, I suppose that's better than nothing. If you do pick up on something, don't be shy," he said grinning. "Is John in his kitchen? He left the rest of the food from the party, and the other policemen and I devoured everything. I want to thank him and particularly tell him what a hit those little brisket sandwiches were. On top of the sweet rolls, I don't know how many of those I had. I'll be back in a few minutes." He stood up and walked over to John's kitchen.

Laura set her coffee cup down and in a serious tone of voice said, "Marty, you're going to hear something about the case today that's going to be very important. I don't know what it is, but keep your ears open. I believe you said you were going back to Mr. Rutledge's house today. Was that his decision or yours?"

"It was his. I specifically suggested he put off the appraisal for awhile, but he wanted to get it over with. I think, although he'll never forget that he met Pia at an antique show, he really doesn't want to stretch out the appraisal because it's how thy met, and anything connected with antiques will remind him of her. He may hope that aspect will fade with time. I could be wrong, but I know I'd feel that way. Speaking of which, I better get going."

Jeff walked out of John's house and said, "John promised me he'd make those little sandwiches for us. Trust me, they're killer." He turned to Marty. "Are you off to the appraisal?"

"Yes, I told Jack I'd be there this morning at ten. On the way there I'm going to stop by the Hi-Lo Drugstore and leave some photos for Lucy to develop since time is critical. I usually send them to her using my computer, but I'm going to pass right by the drugstore, so I'll just stop in and give them to her instead. I'm hoping I can do the art pottery appraisal in one day, since it looks like the dimensions, physical conditions, and descriptions of all of the pieces were noted in the earlier appraisal. That would save a lot of time. I'd think Jack would want to be alone, given all that's happened."

"You do that. I'm going to see if I can sleep for a little while," Jeff said. "I have a meeting with Jack's security guard and his administrative assistant, Nicky, this afternoon. I want to go over the guest list with them, and I also want to discuss it with Jack. There may be a name on the list that rings a bell, or maybe a name he's never heard of. See you later."

"I'm taking Duke out for a walk. Maybe you could do the same when you wake up." She looked at Les and Laura. "I really hate to ask, but if Jeff and I get tied up and it looks like Duke needs to go outside, would one of you help?"

"Laura, my love," Les said, "Marty's your sister. What if someone were to come here to look at one of my paintings I'm selling for $125,000 and they find the artist walking a dog in pink booties in the desert? They'd probably have me committed, and I sure wouldn't make a sale," he said as he walked into his house.

"Duke, don't worry. I'll take care of you," Laura said patting the big dog on the head.

CHAPTER FOURTEEN

"Well, lookie, lookie. If it ain't the appraisal lady that brings me them purty pictures," Lucy said as she looked up from her computer. "Ain't seen you fer awhile. That was one good eatfest at yer' reception. Them boys from The Red Pony food truck did a mighty fine job of fixin' good eats for all of us celebratin' ya' getting' hitched. The ol' man and I couldn't even eat no dinner that night we was so dang stuffed."

Marty had been having her appraisal photos developed at the Hi-Lo Drugstore ever since she'd moved to the high desert. Although Lucy was a bona fide character, she'd become one of Marty's favorite people in the high desert community. She'd even taken care of Duke when everyone from the compound had stayed in motor homes at the country music festival to help John out with his food truck.

"How's that bootie-wearin' dog of yours?" Lucy asked.

"Duke's fine, although he still won't go into the desert without his booties. Did you ever get a dog? I know you were talking about it."

"Land sakes. It has been awhile since we jawed. Yeah, we got a little black puppy. Not real sure what gene pool he comes from. Got him at the county rescue shelter. Cutest little thing you've ever seen. Swore we wouldn't let him up on the furniture. Lady at the shelter said that dogs respect authority and rules. My ol' man didn't pay much attention to that, and first thing I know, he's got that pup in bed with him, and they're both sawin' wood. Now the pup, we named him Herman, don't ask me why, thinks all the furniture is fair game, and we ain't got the chops to tell him he's not allowed to get on it."

"I'll have to pay you a visit. I'd love to see him. Think he's going to be a big dog or a little dog?"

"Well, let me put it this way. If he grows to the size of his paws, the ol' man and me is both gonna have to get us second jobs jes' to feed him, but man, is he ever cute. And them puppy kisses. Well, it's a good thing we ain't never had kids, cuz if the way we're raisin' Herman is any indication, he's gonna be the most spoiled dog in the desert."

"Lucy, to change the subject. When do you think you can get these photos developed? I'm under a real tight time line with this appraisal, and I sure would appreciate it if you could do it sooner rather than later."

"No prob. I'll have them for you by five today. By the way, found this in my daily quote book. Sure says how I feel 'bout that cute little Herman. Here 'tis, 'There is no psychiatrist in the world like a puppy licking your face.' Leastways that's what I think."

"You just may have something there. I'll swing by on my way home tonight and pick up the photos. You'll enjoy them. Some of the most beautiful pieces I've ever seen. See you this afternoon."

*****

After she left the Hi-Lo Drugstore, Marty drove to the polo club and Jack's house. When she entered the lane that led to the house and grounds she saw four florist vans parked near the security guard shack. She waited behind them as each one took two or three large floral arrangements out of the back of their van and put them on a golf cart. She watched the driver of the cart drive up the lane to Jack's house.

I guess I shouldn't be surprised. Pia's death has probably been on the news, and since he's a VIP in Palm Springs, it makes sense people would send floral arrangements. Poor guy.

She knocked on the door of the big house and was greeted by Lupe. "Please come in. Mr. Rutledge is in the library."

"How is he doing?" Marty asked.

"Jensen was able to get him to take a sleeping pill, so I believe he had some sleep. He's just so terribly sad. I've been working for him ever since he came to Palm Springs, and I've never seen him like this. I wish there was something I could do." As they walked down the hall, every room Marty passed was filled with floral arrangements. Lupe opened the door of the library and said, "Mr. Rutledge, Mrs. Combs is here."

"Marty, come in, please. I had Lupe bring all of the art pottery pieces to the library. I thought it would make it easier for you. Here's the appraisal that was done before. Is there anything else you need from me?"

"No. I was going to have you walk me through them, but this looks pretty thorough. I'm curious where you're going to put the art glass collection. I made a mental note that you should secure the pieces with the sticky putty that museums use."

"I don't know. Right now it's too painful for me to look at the pieces. Lupe boxed them up. They're in Pia's suite. I know I'll have to do something with them, but I'm not ready to yet. It's really all I have left of her. By the way, I do have some of that putty, because I use it to secure my art pottery pieces."

"Jack, I wish there was something I could do to ease your pain. I know it sounds trite, but the passing of time will help."

"Thanks, Marty, but that's a pretty hard concept to wrap my head around right now. I just want to get through the next few days. The last two months have been the happiest of my life, and now with Pia gone I'm looking at a very bleak future. I really can't even think straight right now. I need to make some phone calls. Let Taffy know when you're ready for lunch. I'd join you, but the mere thought of food makes me sick right now."

"Thank you, Jack, and I'll try to do this as fast as I can. I'm sure you'd like to be alone."

"Not necessarily. Right now it's probably better for me to keep busy. Let me know before you leave."

CHAPTER FIFTEEN

Marty spent the morning looking at one exquisite art pottery piece after another. Each one was a collector's dream. Rookwood, George Ohr, Heino, Voulkos, Otto Nazler, Beatrice Wood, Fulper, Van Briggle and others fought for her attention. She found it hard to believe that a collection like Jack's existed in a private individual's home. She hoped he'd installed a very good security system. Art theft was not unusual and between the art glass collection and the art pottery collection, the home of Jack Rutledge would certainly be a tempting target.

She looked at her watch and realized it was already one in the afternoon. She'd been appraising for enough years to know when she needed to take a break. She was starting to lose the laser-like focus she needed to be effective. Marty walked down the hall to the kitchen and knocked on the door. Taffy opened it and said, "Mrs. Combs, I've been expecting you. Lupe said you'd be eating lunch here. One of Mr. Rutledge's favorite dishes is a lasagna that's made the night before. I made one late yesterday before the tragedy involving Ms. Marshall happened. He told me he's not hungry, so I hope you'll have some. I made a light salad to go along with it as well as some garlic bread. I'll have the lasagna on the table in five minutes, but the salad is ready right now."

"That sounds wonderful, Taffy. Thank you. How are you doing with everything that's happened around here?"

"I'm fine. I just feel really sorry for Mr. Rutledge. He's been so happy lately. Anyone could see how much in love he was with Mrs. Marshall. I don't know what will happen to him now." It sounded like she muttered something under her breath, but Marty couldn't make out what she said.

"I'm sorry, I thought you said something else, but I didn't pick it up."

Taffy put a spinach salad on the table and said, "I don't think everyone was quite as sorry as Mr. Rutledge that Mrs. Marshall won't be around anymore."

"What do you mean by that?" Marty asked as she sat down and put her napkin in her lap. She took a bite of her spinach salad and said, "This is wonderful, Taffy. One of the men who lives in the compound where I live is a chef. He's the one who did the catering last night, I think he'd love to have the recipe for this salad. Is there any chance I could have it?"

"Certainly. I'll run off a copy for you. Sometimes with the desert heat, there's nothing like a good salad."

"Thanks. Taffy, you didn't answer my question by what you meant when you said not everyone would be as sorry as Mr. Rutledge was that Mrs. Marshall wouldn't be around anymore."

"I shouldn't have said anything. Just pretend you didn't hear it."

"Taffy, I can't. A woman has been murdered, and my husband is in charge of the criminal investigation of the case. If you know anything, please tell me."

Taffy took a deep breath and said, "All of us who work here for Mr. Rutledge were so glad to see him happy, with the exception of Lupe. I think if you talk to anyone at the polo club, they'd agree with me that she's in love with Mr. Rutledge. I saw the looks she gave Mrs. Marshall when she didn't think anyone was looking, and they weren't very nice. I think she's happy Mrs. Marshall is gone."

Marty's hand, which was holding a piece of garlic bread stopped in mid-air, halfway to her mouth, as she asked incredulously, "Are you saying you think Lupe could have murdered Mrs. Marshall because she's in love with Jack Rutledge?"

"No, I would never say anything like that. I'm just saying that I don't think Lupe will be very sorry that Mr. Rutledge won't be marrying Mrs. Marshall. She's changed in the last few months. She's told me she gets really bad headaches. I wonder if she has some medical problem."

Marty finished her lunch digesting not only the food but what Taffy had just told her. She had a hard time equating the soft spoken small Mexican woman with murder, but she knew it was definitely something Jeff needed to know.

*****

Refreshed from her lunch break, Marty went back to the library to continue her appraisal of Jack's art pottery collection. Whenever she was appraising, she tried to block out extraneous sounds, so she could give her full attention to the appraisal. She was vaguely aware of the doorbell ringing and didn't pay much attention to it other than thinking it was interrupting her ability to fully concentrate on what she was doing.

She walked over to the library door intending to close it and heard a woman's voice telling Lupe she was Pia's sister, and she wanted to speak with Jack. Marty stopped when she got to the door and listened, curious as to what Pia's sister would have to say to him. In a moment she heard Gerta say, "I'm Pia's sister, Gerta Martelli. I heard the horrible news about Pia on the news this morning. I can't believe it. Can you tell me anything about what happened?"

"It's nice to meet you, Gerta," Jack said, "although I would rather it wasn't under these circumstances. I was looking forward to meeting you at the cocktail party last night, but we must have missed each other. Please, come into my office."

A moment later she heard Gerta say, "I was at the party, but I left early. I thought I might have a touch of food poisoning. When you're traveling, you often have to eat whatever's available, and the sandwich I had at lunch was not the best. Anyway, I'm sorry for both of our losses. My sister and I had become quite close in the last few years. I'm going to miss her terribly."

"So am I," Jack said softly. "Pia was a wonderful woman. I simply don't understand why anyone would want to murder her. It makes no sense."

"I agree, although I wouldn't be surprised if it was her ex-husband. I heard he was released from prison a few weeks ago. I'm sure the people investigating the murder have already talked to him."

Jack was quiet for a moment and then said, "Gerta, I don't know what you're talking about. I knew Pia had been married and that it wasn't a happy marriage, but I didn't know her ex-husband was in prison."

"I'm not surprised. It wasn't something she was very proud of. The family knew what a loser he was, and that's why none of us had anything to do with her for a long time."

"What was he in prison for?" Jack asked.

"He was convicted of selling drugs. I still can't believe Pia didn't know anything about it while they were married, but I have to give her credit for divorcing him after she learned that's where he'd gotten his money before and during their marriage."

"I don't think the detective who's in charge of the case knows anything about this. What was her ex-husband's name?"

"Frank Marshall. You probably better tell him Frank was and still is no good. I wouldn't be at all surprised to hear he was responsible for her death. You know, she and I were very close. When our mother died, Pia inherited the art glass collection, and I inherited my mother's home. Pia always told me that if something ever happened to her, she wanted me to have the collection, so it would stay in the family. Knowing her wishes, I rented a U-Haul truck this morning, and I've come to take the art glass collection back to New Jersey with me."

That sure doesn't fit with the conversation I heard between Gerta and Pia last night. What's going on? Marty thought, now very curious as to where this was going to lead.

"I think you're mistaken, Gerta," Jack said. "Pia and I made a mutual decision that if something happened to one of us the other one would inherit everything. It's true that I had substantially more than she did, but I didn't want my wealth to be a barrier between us. It seemed simpler that way. We signed our trusts yesterday. According to the terms of the trust, the art glass collection is now mine. I'll treasure it, because it's really the only thing I have of Pia's. I'm sorry if there's been a misunderstanding."

"You can't really expect me to believe Pia would leave the collection to you?" Gerta said raising her voice. "This was a collection my parents treasured and spent many years assembling, not to mention the large amount of money they invested in it. No, the collection is rightfully mine. I demand you let me take it. I've brought boxes and packing materials with me. Just show me where the pieces are, and I'll start boxing them up."

"Gerta, the collection stays here," Jack said in a firm voice. "I'm honoring your sister's wishes by keeping the collection. I'm going to have to ask you to leave now."

"How dare you? I'll have my attorney sue you for everything you're worth. You have no legal claim to that collection. It rightfully belongs to me now that Pia is gone."

"No," Jack said harshly. "It's mine. If you don't leave right now, I'm going to press this button on my desk and two of my security men will escort you from this room and off the property. I would strongly suggest you leave before that becomes necessary."

The next sound Marty heard was the sound of the front door slamming. She assumed it had been slammed by Gerta on her way out of the Polo House. Marty walked out of the library and into Jack's office. He was looking out the window and appeared to be very shaken by his exchange with Gerta.

"Jack, I couldn't help but overhear your conversation with Gerta. Pia introduced me to her last night, and she was very angry that Pia wouldn't give her the collection, since she didn't think it was fair that Pia had the collection and was also marrying a wealthy man."

"I don't need this right now, Marty," he said. "It's all I can do to hold it together, and now if Pia's sister presents problems that may just put me over the edge." He looked at his watch and said, "Good, I hear the doorbell. That must be Father Lawrence. I've decided to bury Pia here on the grounds. I can't deal with some big spectacle type of funeral, and Father Lawrence is going to be with me tomorrow when I bury her. The only other person who will be attending her funeral, if you want to call it that, is my son, Jensen. By the way, I'm meeting your husband in an hour."

"I assume you're going to tell him about Pia's ex-husband. I'm sure that's something he'd want to know about and want to follow up on."

"I will. We're meeting to go over the guest list. The security guard who was in charge of admitting people last night and my administrative assistant, Nicky, are meeting with us as well. Hopefully, the list will provide some information about who might have killed Pia."

"Jack, you're in very good hands with Jeff. There's not a more capable detective on the police force. He worked all night, and right now he's at home trying to get a couple of hours of sleep. If I can help, let me know."

"Actually, I think you can. I had a call from Dick at the insurance company this morning confirming that the binder was in place, and the art glass was insured. He said my personal property here in the

Polo House was insured, but he didn't think an appraisal had ever been on done it. When I mentioned that the house was pretty much decorated in authentic Arts and Crafts furniture such as Stickley and Mission furniture as well as a number of period decorative items, he became concerned that I was very underinsured. He suggested since you were already here you might as well prepare an appraisal for the furniture and the rest of the decorative items."

"I'd be happy to do the appraisal. Believe me, I've noticed the quality of what you have. I just assumed that an appraisal had already been done," Marty said.

"You might as well come back and continue with your work until it's all finished. You seem to know what you're doing, so just go from room to room and do what's necessary. As long as you're doing the collections, it makes sense to finish up the rest of the things in the house."

"If you're comfortable with me being here during this difficult time, I'd be happy to do it, but I certainly would understand if you wanted to put it off for a few weeks."

"No, let's get it over with. It will be one less thing I have to think about. If you need anything, ask Lupe. I'll be with Father Lawrence and your husband. Jensen is coming here again tonight. He's really been a big help to me. He's pretty much handling everything right now, and with the polo season coming up in a few months, there's so much to do. The time leading up to the season is actually our busiest time. Once the season starts, everything's pretty much on cruise control. I'll see you later," he said as he walked out of the room.

CHAPTER SIXTEEN

Marty finished her appraisal of Jack's art pottery late that afternoon. As she walked to the front door, she heard Jeff's voice coming from Jack's study and at the same time saw his unmarked police car parked in the driveway.

That's a long meeting. Hope Jeff's able to find something out.

She was about halfway home when her phone rang. She pressed the Bluetooth button and saw that the caller was Jeff. "Good afternoon, my love. How did the meeting with Jack go?"

"It went well. I need to go to the station and make some calls. Between Jack and the security gate guard we have a couple of leads. I'll tell you all about it tonight. I should be there in about an hour. Tell John if I'm late to start without me."

"Right. You know how well that goes over with him. While having a resident chef prepare gourmet dinners is an asset, having a resident chef who takes offense if anyone is late to his dinner is a liability. I think you and John are going to have to come to a meeting of the minds on that issue, because I'm sure there are times when you're definitely going to be late, and he's going to have to get used to it."

"I agree. I'll have a talk with him. I just pulled into the station, so I'll see you later. I love you."

"Love you too. I'm on my way to the Hi-Lo Drugstore. I need to pick up the photos I left with Lucy this morning. The art glass appraisal is my number one priority because of the binder. It's for one week only, and I don't want to be the one responsible for that collection not being insured. Jack asked me to appraise everything in the house that has value, so I'll probably be working late a few nights. You can remind me of that the next time you have to work nights," she said laughing. "See you later."

*****

"Well if it ain't my favorite appraiser lady. Man, them pictures were somethin' else. Hard to believe somebody gots all them purties in one place," Lucy said as she handed Marty a bag filled with the photograph prints made from the disc Marty had left with her to be developed that morning.

"Thanks for the quick service, Lucy. I really appreciate it. I have six more days to get this appraisal done, so I'm really tight on time. Here are my photos from today, but there's no rush on these. I would have sent them from my computer, but since I was coming here anyway, I thought I'd just drop them off with you."

"Went home at lunchtime and took a coupla of pics of Herman fer ya'. Knew you'd want to see my little guy," Lucy said. "Man, has he got sharp teeth. Be glad when he's outta the puppy stage. Nothin' is safe. I got puppy tooth marks on my readin' glasses, the television remote control, and my phone. You name it, and it's probably got little tooth marks on it. To say nothin' of my toes. If I could clone my toes and sell 'em to people with puppies, I'd retire a rich woman. My toes seem to be Herman's favorite things to chew on." She handed the puppy photos to Marty.

"Mercifully, those days are behind me. I'd forgotten about the toes. Guess they're about on a puppy's eye level. Maybe that's the reason for their fascination with them," Marty said laughing. She looked at the photographs Lucy had handed to her. "What a little darling. Any time you want me to return the favor you did for me by keeping Duke, I'd be happy to keep Herman for you."

"Thanks. I'll keep it in mind. Jes' one sec before ya' go. Gotta share my latest puppy thing with ya'. Got it off the Internet this afternoon. Ready?"

"Sure. What did you find?"

"Here it is, 'Acquiring a dog may be the only time a person gets to choose a relative.' Don't know 'bout you, Marty, but me and my ol' man got some relatives that would make the nastiest junkyard dog seem like a saint by comparison. Kind of reminded me of some quote I heard once 'bout how ya' can pick yer friends but ya' can't pick yer' family. Lotta truth there, don't ya' think?"

"Sheer wisdom, Lucy, sheer wisdom," Marty said as she thought of Pia and her sister Gerta. "Again, thanks for the quick service." She walked out to her car and drove the rest of the way to the compound while she slowly reviewed in her mind the events of the last two days.

CHAPTER SEVENTEEN

"Hi everyone, let me take Duke out, and I'll be back in a few minutes," Marty said as she greeted John, Max, Laura, and Les who were seated around the courtyard picnic table having a glass of wine.

"No need to, Marty. He and I just got back from a walk," Laura said. "I thought you might be a little rushed with your appraisal and everything that's taken place. Put your stuff away and then come join us."

"Back in a minute. Sounds good. By the way, Jeff called, and he has to go to the station to make a couple of calls, but he said he'd be here within an hour. John, he specifically wanted you to know that he's hurrying."

"I appreciate that. When I was in Italy several years ago I took a cooking class from an Italian chef, and her favorite saying was, 'Pasta waits for no man.' I've kind of adopted it and changed it to 'My dinner waits for no man,' but given Jeff's profession, I'm probably going to have to ease up on that rule as it applies to him," John said laughing.

"I'm sure he'd be very appreciative. He's got enough on his mind at the moment."

Marty walked into her house, deposited the sack with the appraisal photos on her desk, and changed clothes. She walked out to the courtyard and said, "Les, I'd love a glass of wine from that lovely looking bottle of chilled white wine you have in front of you. It's been a long and hectic day."

"We were just talking about the murder, and we're all curious what happened today. Want to tell us or do you want to wait for Jeff?" Laura asked.

"Let's wait. No sense repeating everything. Actually, you're not going to have to wait very long, because I think I just saw Jeff's car pull into the driveway." She stood up and walked to the gate. A moment later Jeff greeted her with a hug and a kiss.

"Let me change clothes, and I'll be with you all in a minute."

*****

Jeff returned a few minutes later casually dressed in shorts and a T-shirt. "There's something pretty freeing about taking that gun off, believe me," he said as he poured himself a glass of wine. "Since I only got a few hours of sleep today, I really need to catch up tonight. Maybe this glass of wine will ease the way."

"Jeff, we've been waiting to hear what's happening with the Pia Marshall murder case. Any leads yet?" John said.

"Possibly. A couple of interesting things happened this afternoon. Marty, I believe you overheard Pia's sister tell Jack that Pia had been married to Frank Marshall, a felon who was just released from prison a couple of weeks ago."

"You're kidding!" Les said. "Did Rutledge know about it?"

"From what he told me, no. He said Gerta told him the murderer was probably Pia's ex-husband. Then he said she demanded that he give her the art glass collection that Pia inherited from her parents."

"Are you serious? That's pretty brutal considering the poor guy's fiancée was just murdered," Laura said.

"I'll vouch for it. I was in the library appraising Jack's art pottery collection when I heard her come in. I was going to close the door to the library, but I couldn't help but overhear what she was saying. Being the brazen snoop that I am, I stood there and listened. He told her he wouldn't be giving her the collection, because Pia had signed a trust two days ago giving it to him. Gerta was furious. He told her to leave, or he'd call his security guards." Marty turned to Jeff. "Do you think that makes Gerta a suspect?"

"She is in my book. She definitely had a motive for killing Pia – the art glass collection which, don't forget, is worth several million dollars. That, plus the fact she was at the cocktail party last night puts her near the top of my list of suspects, but as always, naming a suspect is one thing, proving they committed a murder is another."

"Jeff, what are you doing about Pia's ex-husband? I would think he'd be a suspect just because he served time in prison," Les said.

"Of course my antenna went way up when Jack told me that little tidbit of information. One of the reasons I had to go back to the station tonight was to call a friend of mine in Los Angeles. He and I went to the police academy together years ago, and we've stayed friends and kept in touch. I've helped him out a couple of times, and he's helped me out as well. He's going to see what he can find out from Frank's parole officer. He's also going to try and find out where Frank was last night."

"Hey, everybody. I really want to hear what Jeff has to say about the other interesting things that happened today. Okay with you if we eat a bit late tonight?" John asked.

"Only if I have permission to be late from time to time," Jeff said grinning at John.

"Permission granted. Now what else was interesting?" John asked.

"I met with Jack, his administrative assistant, and the security guard who was at the guard shack during the cocktail party. It was an interesting setup. Each guest had an invitation with their name on it. They gave it to the guard who took a picture of it along with the guest." He looked at Marty. "Remember how angry Jack got when the guard called him last night and told him he thought he'd recognized Kevin Sanders, but he had an invitation with a different name on it?"

"Yes. I remember."

"Well, the guard was right. When Jack compared the man's photo with the name on the invitation, he positively identified the man as being Kevin Sanders. Evidently the name on the invitation belonged to a doctor who had invested in Jack's polo team last year and couldn't attend the party, because he had to be on duty at the hospital. The doctor knows Kevin Sanders, and asked him if he needed another invitation. He didn't know about the bad blood between Jack and Kevin. My problem with Sanders is the same as my problem with Pia's sister, Gerta. Kevin was evidently at the cocktail party, but there is no evidence to link him to the murder."

"I seem to remember seeing the name Kevin Sanders in the papers over the years. He's a bigwig in the polo world, isn't he?" Laura asked.

"Yes. From what Jack told me that's the reason for the bad blood between them. He was the number one polo guy in Palm Springs before Jack moved here. There was an old polo club where Kevin played. Jack came to town and built this state of the art polo club and along with it, made his team the best in the United States and maybe the world. He thinks his team is that good."

"What does Kevin do now?" Marty asked.

"He has his own polo team, but his team has definitely become second rate compared to Jack's. From what Jack told me, he blames Jack for him now being considered a 'has-been' player. He can't get investors, and he can't get good players. Everyone prefers to be with Jack."

"Sounds like a motive to me," Les said.

"Yes, so now we have as possible suspects Jack's son, Jensen, Gerta, Kevin, and Frank," Jeff said. "And I'd be remiss if I didn't mention Jack as a suspect."

"What?" they said, almost in unison. Marty was the first to speak. "Jeff, you can't be serious! His wife-to-be was the woman who was murdered. What possible motive would he have for killing her?"

"Marty, easy. You're the one who told me Pia's art glass collection was probably worth several million dollars. Any time that much money is on the table, it becomes a motive."

"Jeff, I know you're the detective, but I don't see Jack Rutledge as a murderer. You may have him on the list, but I think he should be at the very bottom."

"So noted, Marty, but I'm keeping him on the list. There's one other thing that was interesting. One of the names on the guest list was a man by the name of Luigi Marco. Jack doesn't know him, but his administrative assistant said a man, obviously Italian, called last week and said he was interested in possibly becoming an investor in Jack's polo team. He said he couldn't come to the cocktail party because of a prior commitment, but he'd like to send one of his employees, and the employee could report back to him. Nicky kept a record of everyone who had been sent an invitation, and she'd sent it to a man by the name of Roberto Battisto. He'd asked that the invite be sent to him but issued in the name of Luigi Marco."

"I'd think Jack would be thrilled to have people interested in becoming sponsors," Les said.

"Yes and no. We maintain a large database at the station of known Mafia members. It may be profiling, but any time someone with an Italian name is connected to a crime, we run it through that database. Nothing came up on Luigi, but Battisto's rumored to be the West Coast Mafia Family's number two man. According to what I found out, his uncle is now the head of it, and Battisto will be taking over the Family business in the future." He sat back and sipped his wine while they digested the information.

"Are you saying he could be a possible suspect?" John asked.

"I think the timing is interesting. Jack says he never met the man, and he doesn't know Battisto. The problem with Marco is motive. What could possibly be his motive? I'm having my friend in Los Angeles check out that angle as well. I'm hopeful we'll have something tomorrow. Oh, one more thing. Marty, I don't think I told you this morning that a cigarette was found next to Pia's body."

Marty interrupted him. "It probably was Pia's. She told me she was trying to give up smoking, but she felt she could justify one cigarette. When she left to go outside she said the last hour had been stressful for her, and she wanted to have a cigarette. What did you find out about it?"

"You're right. Although DNA tests usually take weeks, once in a while I can request that one be done on an emergency basis. Pia's DNA was found on the cigarette. What's interesting about it is she must have just lit the cigarette when she was murdered, because it didn't look like more than a couple of puffs had been taken on it. I was able to get fingerprints other than Pia's off of it."

"Do you think the fingerprints are those of the murderer?" Marty asked.

"Possibly, very possibly, but it may not do us any good because although the prints are clear, I ran them through the national fingerprint databank, and there was no match."

"What does that mean?" Max asked.

"It means the person whose fingerprints are on the cigarette has never been printed by any law enforcement agency which tells me the person doesn't have a criminal record. Essentially, the fingerprints are of absolutely no value to us at this time."

They were all quiet processing what Jeff had just told them. Laura was the first to speak. "Jeff, I know you've become somewhat of a believer in whatever psychic gift I have. Here's what I'm getting. I'm sensing a lot of feminine energy surrounding Pia's death. I know you have a number of male suspects, but I'm not getting that kind of energy."

"Well, if you're right, and you usually are, that means Gerta must be the murderer. She's the only woman we've identified as a suspect. Does that sound right to you?" he asked.

"I can't say for sure, and I could be wrong. The only solid thing I'm getting is that it's none of the men you've been discussing."

"Maybe it will be a little clearer as we begin a process of elimination," Jeff said. "I expect to know something tomorrow."

"Jeff, if you're pretty much through giving us an update on the murder investigation, Max and I need to put the finishing touches on dinner."

"John, with the past twenty-four hours I've had, I'll be fine with whatever you bring out. What are we having tonight?" Jeff asked.

"Something new for me. It's a crab mac and cheese pasta. The reason I want to try it out on all of you is I think I could make it ahead of time and put it in little ramekins and then heat them in the microwave when someone places an order for it. Since more and more people like to try a couple of things for lunch, this could be my version of a small plate at the food trucks. Back in a couple of minutes."

*****

"John, this is a no-brainer. Anyone who wouldn't like this dish doesn't deserve to eat at your food truck. It's wonderful and definitely worth five stars," Marty said. She looked around the table. "Don't you all agree?"

The answer was a resounding yes. Within minutes the table was cleared, and everyone headed to their own home. It had been a long, long day.

A few minutes later Marty closed the door to their house and said, "Jeff, why don't you go to bed? I can tell from that vacant look in your eyes you're out on your feet. I really do need to do a little work on the art glass appraisal."

"Thanks for being so understanding. This wasn't quite how I wanted to start our married life, but unfortunately, I didn't have a choice. What's on your agenda tomorrow? Finishing up the art glass appraisal?"

"No. I'm going back to Jack's. Like I said earlier, I have to appraise all of the rest of the things in his house I consider to be of value. It really puts me under the gun to complete this appraisal. I'll be in bed in a couple of hours. As I told you, a lot of this appraisal is simply going to be my judgment call on values. I just hope he never has a loss, and I'm never challenged. Good night, sweetheart. I love you."

"Marty, I'd like to say I'll be gallant and wait up for you, but we both know that isn't going to happen. See you in the morning," he said as he turned off the light.

CHAPTER EIGHTEEN

Lupe opened the front door of Jack's house and walked along a narrow gravel path that led to her apartment behind the garage. She was glad Jensen would be staying with his father again tonight. She'd also be glad when they buried Pia tomorrow and things in the Rutledge house could get somewhat back to normal.

She opened the door of her apartment, luxuriating in the spaciousness of it. When she was a child growing up in a small village in Mexico, Lupe, along with her brothers and sisters, slept with her parents in their one room hovel. There were no beds, only a makeshift sleeping area. They huddled together for warmth in the winters, substituting their body heat for a non-existent furnace or fireplace. Her father desperately wanted to give his children a better life than he and her mother had, and one day he told his young family that they were going to move to the United States. He said he'd given all his money to a man who promised he would take them there using a special secret route he knew about.

It turned out the secret route hadn't been so secret, and it didn't help that the man had been on the payroll of the American border patrol. The van they were riding in had been filled with illegal immigrants trying to sneak across the border into the United States, and when it had been stopped at the roadblock set by the border patrol, everyone in her family had been taken into custody and sent back to Mexico. The only thing that kept Lupe from being sent back was the flashlight the border patrol guard had shined in the van. The battery died before the light could illuminate Lupe who was huddled in a corner far away from the door. The guard had to get a new battery from his car, and she had just enough time to slip out of the van and hide behind some desert scrub plants before he returned.

While she changed out of her maid's uniform and into a pair of sweat pants and a T-shirt, she thought back to the years following her escape from Mexico. She'd made her way to San Diego without food or water. For several days she lived on what she could find on the streets and in garbage cans. She couldn't remember how she'd done it, only that she had. Aimlessly walking the streets after several nights of sleeping in doorways, she'd seen a Catholic Church. She'd knocked on the door, and it had been opened by a nun as round as she was tall with a glorious sunny smile on her face.

The nun had called Lupe "Nina," and gently pulled her into the church. She spoke perfect Spanish and wanted to know how Lupe had come to the church. Lupe told her everything that had happened since she'd left her small village in Mexico. Shortly, Lupe was sitting at a table with more food in front of her than she'd had in days. She gulped the food down and drank three glasses of milk. When she was finished the nun led her to small room with a bed in it, told her to sleep, and that she'd be back for her in the morning.

For the first time in days Lupe felt safe. She had no idea what the future held for her, but she knew it couldn't be any worse that what had happened since she'd left the village. The next morning the nun told her she was going to ride in a bus to a town called Palm Springs. The nun had said there was a Catholic home there for Mexican children who needed a place to live in the United States. She'd told Lupe she'd be safe there with plenty of food and a bed of her own.

Thirty-three children had lived with her in the Catholic home in Palm Springs whose funding came from a diocese in Los Angeles. She was taught to read and write in the small school maintained in the home. When she was eighteen she went to work as a live-in maid for a wealthy donor to the Catholic home. Lupe worked for her for five years. About that time the woman decided to move back to Los

Angeles, having grown to intensely dislike the hot desert summers.

The woman was very wealthy, and when Jack Rutledge had come to Palm Springs to build his home and start his polo club, he was introduced to the woman. She liked him and had invested money in his polo team. Since she was getting ready to leave Palm Springs, she asked him if he would hire Lupe. She said she could personally vouch for her because Lupe had worked for her for five years. That was ten years ago. She'd loved being the maid at the Polo House and thought she was the luckiest person in the world to work for Jack Rutledge.

She sat down at the kitchen table and booted up the computer Jack had given her several years ago for Christmas. She'd learned how to use it and now she pulled up the names and phone numbers of different places that might be interested in taking some of the floral arrangements that had been sent to the home. At the last count there were over fifty of them scattered throughout the house. Jack had asked her to find a place for them, and she'd instructed the guards to take them down to the security guard shack so vans from the various retirement homes and other similar places could pick them up.

Lupe fixed a bowl of soup and a sandwich for dinner and thought again how nice it would be to have the funeral out of the way tomorrow. Hopefully Jack would feel better once that was behind him.

She washed her dishes and then prepared for her favorite time of day. Several years earlier Lupe had read about the benefit of meditation, and it had fascinated her. She'd tried it as a way to escape the almost crippling headaches she'd started to have. At first she'd only have a few headaches a year, but lately they'd become more intense and more frequent. When she was meditating in her special room with the shrine she'd made, she escaped them. She opened the door and walked into the small room she used when she meditated and lit three candles, one for her, one for the spirit, and one that she wished on. She sat down on her small decorative pillow and looked around the room, smiling at the secret place she'd created, knowing for a few hours she'd have relief from her headaches.

CHAPTER NINETEEN

Promptly at ten Marty knocked on the front door of the Polo House and it was quickly opened by Lupe. "Buenos Dias," Marty said as she walked in. "Don't be concerned if you see me going from room to room today. Mr. Rutledge wants me to appraise the rest of the items in the house that I think need to be evaluated. I'm sure I won't be able to finish today, so I'll probably be back tomorrow."

"That's fine. Mr. Rutledge told me to tell you if you need anything to let me know. I think it will be a little easier to work today, because I have arranged for the floral arrangements to be given to some retirement homes and other places that might enjoy them. I imagine it would be difficult for you to try and concentrate on the different pieces when there are so many floral arrangements causing distractions."

"That was very thoughtful of you," Marty said.

"It was Mr. Rutledge's idea. He is so wonderful. He is with Father Stevenson now. They are burying Ms. Marshall. I hope he will be happier when that's over with."

You hope he'll be happier when that's over with? What a strange thing to say, Marty thought.

"Taffy will serve you lunch. Is there anything I can do for you?"

Lupe asked.

"No. I think I'll start in the living room. He has some very fine Arts and Crafts furniture and decorative items in there. Thanks anyway." Marty walked into the living room and slowly began to make her way from piece to piece, photographing, measuring, and assessing the condition of each item. It was a time-consuming process, but one that couldn't be hurried.

Marty was aware that Jack, Father Stevenson, and Jensen had returned to the house. She heard them go into Jack's study and close the door. She blocked out the sounds of the phone and doorbell ringing as more floral arrangements were delivered. She heard Lupe tell one of the guards who brought the arrangements to the house to keep any future ones at the guard shack and give the cards on them to Jack's administrative assistant, Nicky, so she could properly acknowledge them.

"Excuse me, Mrs. Combs. It's 12:30, and I thought you might like some lunch," Taffy said.

"I would love some, thank you. I need to take a measurement of this painting, and then I'll be through in this room. Be there in a minute."

When Marty walked into the kitchen the table had been set with coral linens the color the desert sky sometimes gets at dusk. Several vases were filled with brightly colored flowers giving the room a cheery ambiance. A bowl of what looked like chilled cucumber soup was on the table with a loaf of warm sourdough bread next to it. Butter had been softened in a white ramekin dish and a glass of iced tea had been placed directly in front of her knife.

"Taffy, this looks wonderful. Thank you so much. You wouldn't think someone could get hungry just looking at beautiful things and taking photographs, but I seem to always be starving when I'm appraising." She took a spoonful of the soup and said, "This is wonderful. I know you gave me a recipe yesterday, but I'm wondering if I would be wearing out my welcome if I asked you for this one as well."

"Of course, Mrs. Combs. I'll copy it right now for you." She left and returned a few moments later with the recipe and handed it to Marty. She seemed distracted and nervous, moving from one side of the kitchen to the other. She washed and dried a few dishes. Marty watched her, unsure of what she should do. It was quite apparent to her that the Taffy she was with today was not the same woman she'd been with yesterday.

Finally, Marty couldn't stand it any longer. She set her spoon down and the piece of bread she had in her hand and said, "Taffy, I may be overstepping my bounds here, but is something wrong? You seem really nervous and agitated."

Taffy turned around and faced her. "I found something today, and I don't know what I should do about it."

"All right. Why don't you tell me about it, and perhaps I can help?"

"I know your husband's the detective who's trying to find out who killed Mrs. Marshall. He talked to all of us here at the house yesterday. He said to call him if we thought of anything that might be tied to the murder. I found something today, but I don't want to bother him if it's nothing. It scares me."

"What is it, Taffy? Do you have it?" Marty asked.

Taffy pulled what looked like a newspaper clipping out of her pocket and handed it to Marty. Marty looked at it and audibly gasped. "Taffy, where did you find this?" she asked.

Taffy told her about the small servant's room down the hall and how it was sometimes used as a backup pantry for duplicate kitchen items. She paused and took a sip of water. "When I couldn't find the coffee that I know is Mr. Rutledge's favorite, I looked for some in the servant's room. I found the clipping you're looking at in there. I took the newspaper clipping from the room and put it in my purse, and then I went to the store and bought his coffee. Well, actually I didn't buy it. I put it on the charge account the Polo House has there. When I got back here an hour ago I didn't know what to do. I thought about showing it to Mr. Rutledge, but he was in his office with his son and Father Stevenson. That's all I know."

"Taffy, you don't need to worry about it. I think it would be wise not to mention what you found to Mr. Rutledge. It would only upset him. My husband's police station isn't too far from here. I want to run this over to him. If anyone asks where I am, just tell them I needed to get a battery for my camera. I'll be back shortly, and thanks again for lunch. It was fabulous."

Marty pushed her chair back and walked to the living room where she'd left her equipment. She put her camera in her case, grabbed her purse, and walked out the front door to her car.

CHAPTER TWENTY

As soon as Marty got in her car she called Jeff to tell him she was on her way to the police station and needed to talk to him. She heard his voicemail pick up and his familiar voice saying, "This is Detective Combs. I can't take your call right now. If this is an emergency, please hang up and dial 911, otherwise, leave a message, and I'll get back to you as soon as possible."

She left a message and hoped he was at the station. A few minutes later she parked in the visitor's parking lot and hurried into the lobby. She stopped at the reception desk and said, "I'm Marty Combs, Detective Combs' wife. If he's in, I'd like to talk to him for a few minutes."

"Please have a seat, Mrs. Combs, and I'll see if he's available." She picked up her phone while Marty walked over to a nearby bench and sat down. Moments later the receptionist motioned to her and said, "He'll be with you in a moment. He's on another phone call and asked you to wait here."

Five minutes later the door behind the receptionist opened and Jeff walked out and over to Marty. "This is a surprise. I'm not sure you've ever dropped into the station like this. Are you all right?"

"I'm fine, Jeff. I left a voicemail for you, but you probably haven't had time to check your phone for messages. I have something I need to show you, and I think it might be important to Pia's murder case."

"Sounds interesting. Follow me to my office. It's quieter in there." They walked down a hall, and he motioned for her to go into the office with the words "Detective Combs" on the door. He closed it behind him and pointed for her to sit in the chair opposite his desk.

"So, my love, what's so important that you'd leave an appraisal to come to my office? Somehow I don't think it's just because you missed me."

"Well, I do miss you, but there's more to it than that." She spent the next few minutes telling him about Taffy and the newspaper clipping she'd found and given to Marty.

"Let's see what you've got." He took the piece of paper from her and let out a low whistle. "So she found this attached to the back of a cupboard door in the room that's known as the servant's room, but she has no idea how it got there or who it belongs to. Is that right?"

"Yes. I'm wondering if it has something to do with the murder. What do you think?" Marty asked.

"The one thing I've learned in all of my years of police investigations is not to assume anything or take anything at face value, however this is the first solid clue we've had in the case. I assume you and Taffy both handled this."

"Yes. She gave it to me, and I took it from her. Why?"

"I want to see if I can lift some fingerprints off of it and then run it through the fingerprint databank. Are you going back to the Polo House?"

"Yes, I told Taffy if anyone asked where I was to tell them that I needed to get a battery for my camera. Why?"

"I don't think you're in the fingerprint system, and I have no idea if Taffy is. I'd like to fingerprint both of you, so we can eliminate your fingerprints. The fingerprints of the murderer could very well be on this newspaper clipping. Are you on your way back there now?"

"Yes. What reason will you use for fingerprinting us at the house in case someone sees you doing it?"

"If anyone walks in while I'm doing it I'll just say I've decided to fingerprint everyone at the house in order to eliminate prints, and then I'll take a print of that person. Actually it's a pretty standard procedure, so I doubt if anyone would question it. Go on back to the house. I need to get a portable fingerprint kit from the crime lab, and I'll meet you there in a few minutes."

When Marty got back to the Polo House it was quiet. She rang the doorbell, but Lupe didn't answer. After a moment, she tried the door, and finding it unlocked, she let herself in and walked to the kitchen. Taffy was listening to the television while she was stirring something in a large bowl.

"I'm back, Taffy. I rang the doorbell, but no one answered, so I let myself in."

"I'm sorry, Mrs. Combs. When Lupe isn't in the house, I'm supposed to answer the door. I was nervous, so I decided to turn on the television to distract me, and when I get nervous I like to cook. It calms me down. Mr. Rutledge loves peanut butter cookies, so I thought I'd make a batch for him. It's not much, but maybe it will help him a little."

"I'm a huge fan of peanut butter cookies myself, so if you have a couple of extra ones, I'd love to have them. I took the newspaper clipping you gave me to my husband, and he's on his way here to fingerprint both of us. He wants to see if he can pick up any fingerprints off the newspaper clipping, and he needs our fingerprints, so we can be eliminated, since both of us touched it."

"Does he think it has something to do with the murder?" Taffy asked, her eyes wide with the knowledge she might have found something that could lead to the murderer.

"He said it was the first solid clue they'd had in the case, so I assume the answer is yes. I hear the doorbell. It's probably Jeff. Do you want me to get it for you?"

"Yes, thanks. I don't like to walk away when I'm in the middle of combining the ingredients in a recipe. It wouldn't be the first time I've doubled an ingredient or assumed I'd already added an ingredient and left it out. Not a good thing for a person who's a cook to do."

Marty walked to the front door and let Jeff in. "Taffy's in the kitchen making peanut butter cookies. I've already claimed a couple for later on today. No one else seems to be around, so I don't think you'll have to explain anything. I've already told Taffy what you'll be doing, and she's expecting you."

"This should only take a few minutes. On my way here there was a message from my friend in Los Angeles. I told him I'd call him when I got back to the station. I'm anxious to see what he's found out."

"So am I. I haven't seen Jack since I got back, so I'm hoping he's feeling well enough to take care of some of his business affairs. He mentioned that the time leading up to the polo season was far more work than the actual season. He said once the season began it was kind of like everything was on cruise control, but even so it has to be hard for him to deal with work related matters right now."

"Marty, I've seen enough of death to know that it's never easy, no matter what the circumstances. I've never decided whether knowing someone was going to die from say, a long illness, was easier than a quick death, which is like a punch to the stomach and knowing your life will never be the same. No, it's never easy," he said as he followed her to the kitchen.

Jeff walked over to Taffy and said, "It's good to see you again, Taffy. Thanks for giving that newspaper clipping to Marty. I think it could be a very important piece of evidence. Marty mentioned she told you I'd be fingerprinting you. All you have to do is put the five fingers of your right hand on this scanner, hold them there for a few seconds, and then repeat it with your left hand. It will automatically record your fingerprints. I'll give this to the police crime lab personnel, and they'll take it from there. It's really very easy."

Taffy put her fingers on the pad and held them where Jeff had indicated. "That's good, Taffy, thanks. Marty, you're next." She did the same. When she was finished Jeff put the small machine back in its case and said, "Thanks, ladies. Marty, I'll see you at home this evening. Taffy, thanks for cooperating, and if you have any extra cookies, you could give a couple to Marty for me," he said grinning, as he walked down the hall to the front door.

CHAPTER TWENTY-ONE

Marty went into the library and started appraising the furniture in that room. She looked at the antique roll-top desk, the Morris chairs, and the other pieces, noting how perfectly the Rookwood lamp she'd seen the first day went with them. She'd been in a lot of antique shops over the years that specialized in furniture from the Arts and Crafts period, but she'd never seen pieces as good as the ones in this room. She knew there was no way she could finish the appraisal today, or possibly even tomorrow. She still had the dining room, Pia's suite, Jack's suite, and his office to appraise. Although she hadn't been in Jack's suite or the dining room, she was certain that the quality of the items in those rooms would be every bit as good as what she'd seen so far.

She finished up the library and made a mental note to call her friend who specialized in antique books. That was an area of antiques, similar to Pre-Columbian art and other specialty areas, that needed someone who was an expert in that field. Marty was a generalist, and although she was very comfortable appraising furniture, glassware, fine art, silver, and ceramics, she knew she'd be doing a disservice to Jack if she attempted to appraise the books in the library.

Taffy knocked lightly on the door. "Taffy, please, come in. I was just getting ready to go into the dining room."

"I thought you could use a little sugar. Here's a couple of the peanut butter cookies I made. Mr. Rutledge came into the kitchen and seemed very happy I'd baked them. He even smiled for the first time in the last couple of days. I'm glad I took the time to make them. Here's a little sack with some cookies in it for your husband. Would you give them to him?"

Marty took a bite of one of the cookies. "This is hands down the best peanut butter cookie I've ever had. If Jeff hadn't seen you making them, I could probably get away with eating all of them myself, but yes, I promise I'll give the sack to him. I'll probably give the other people I live with a taste of the cookies, and I'll bet my friend the chef will ask me if you'll give me the recipe for them. He might have to start a 'From Taffy' section on his menu," she said laughing.

Marty continued, "I should be able to finish the dining room today. I looked in there a few minutes ago, and while everything is just as good as what's in this room, there aren't as many decorative items. It's mainly the table and chairs as well as the china and silver along with a couple of paintings. It shouldn't take me more than an hour and a half. I'll let myself out when I'm finished, and I'll see you tomorrow."

"If your husband finds out anything about that newspaper clipping, would you tell me? It gives me the creeps."

"Of course, Taffy, and I agree. That was really creepy. I didn't even like handling it."

"Me neither. See you tomorrow," she said as she walked out of the room.

Marty finished the items in the dining room and looked at her watch. It was five-thirty. She thought about stopping by to see Earl Mathers, her friend the book appraiser, but decided to give him a call when she got home instead. It had been a long day, and she was ready to take a break. She packed up her appraisal equipment and walked to her car, looking forward to some quiet time during the thirty-minute drive to the compound.

*****

As usual, when she got to the compound Duke was waiting for her at the gate, and the other members of the compound, minus Jeff, were sharing the day's events over a glass of wine at the large table in the courtyard.

She walked over to them and said, "I think you'll like the peanut butter cookies in this sack," as she placed them on the table, "but you have to save two for Jeff. John, I'm pretty sure I can get the recipe for these if you like them, but since it's another one from Taffy, if you decide to serve them at The Pony, I think she should have a little spot on your menu mentioning her by name. I'm taking Duke out for a walk, and then I need to make a call. Back in a few minutes."

When she returned from walking Duke she called Earl, and he told her he could appraise the antique books the following afternoon. Marty was glad he could, because she was anxious to finish up the appraisal of the household items, so she could get to the art glass segment.

"Here you go, Marty," John said handing her a glass of wine. "Figure you could use this after today. We're all anxious to hear if there's anything new on the murder case, but we can wait until Jeff gets here. Any idea when that will be?"

"I saw him this afternoon, and he said he'd see me at home tonight, so I think he should be here pretty soon."

"Marty, how's the art glass portion of the appraisal doing?" Laura asked. "Dick's a little nervous having a binder on a collection for such a large amount when it's never been previously appraised. He knows you're a very good appraiser, but if something happened to that collection, there's no back-up information as to why it's worth that much. He's concerned his head might be on the chopping block if a claim was filed. Alliance Property and Casualty Company wouldn't be very happy if there was a loss, and they didn't have an appraisal for a collection worth that amount."

"Actually there is, Laura. Tell Dick he doesn't need to worry. I have extensive photographs of every piece in the collection with close-ups of marks and conditions. Even if something happened to the whole collection, I have enough back-up information that it would stand up to any challenge. Anyone who knows anything about art glass would almost certainly agree with me that the collection is worth that amount."

"Good. He thinks he's in the beginning stages of getting an ulcer, so that will be one less thing he has to worry about." She looked around, hearing footsteps on the gravel path outside the gate. "Hi, Jeff, we've been waiting for you. Hurry up and change clothes, because we all want to know what's new."

Jeff returned a few minutes later and gratefully accepted the glass of wine John had poured for him. He took a sip and said, "Nectar of the gods! Thanks." He looked at Marty and said, "Did you tell them what happened today?"

She shook her head indicating no.

"Marty, have you been holding out on us? We've been sitting here eagerly waiting for Jeff to tell us what happened, and you knew something and didn't even bother to tell us?" Laura said.

"I didn't feel it was my place to say anything. It's Jeff's case."

Max, John, Laura, and Les turned to Jeff with expectant looks on their faces. "Well, Jeff?" Laura said.

"Taffy, the cook at the Rutledge Polo House, happened to go into the servant's room to see if there was another can of the special type of coffee that Jack likes to drink in the morning. Evidently the room is also used as a second pantry, although Taffy said she rarely goes in there. She said Lupe keeps her purse in there and other personal things she might need. Anyway, when Taffy opened the cabinet which was used for the extra kitchen items she noticed that the door to the cabinet next to it, where Lupe kept her personal items, was partially open.

"She started to close it and saw that a newspaper clipping had been pinned to the inside of the cabinet door. It was an article about Jack and his soon-to-be-wife, Pia, on the society page of the Desert Sun. The article had been cut out of the paper in a large L shape, and the bottom part of the L was a photograph of Pia. Here's the disturbing part. There was a red circle around Pia's face with a red diagonal slash mark drawn through it. It was similar to the kind of 'Do Note Enter' signs you see on the road."

"What happened then?" John asked as all of them leaned forward in anticipation of what Jeff was going to tell them.

"It really disturbed Taffy, so she unpinned it and took it with her. Marty noticed how tense she seemed and commented on it. Taffy showed Marty what she'd found, and Marty brought it to me at the police station. I had the crime lab run tests this afternoon to see if there were any fingerprints on it besides Marty's and Taffy's."

"What were the results, Jeff?" Marty asked.

"The good news is they picked up some fingerprints, however, the bad news is they weren't in the system. When the technician finished, I asked him to see if the fingerprints they found on the newspaper matched the fingerprints on the cigarette we found next to Pia's body." He took another sip of wine.

"And?" Les asked.

"The technician said it was a positive match. Now the problem I have is to figure out whose prints those are."

"So, based on what you told us last night, the person whose fingerprints are on both the newspaper clipping and the cigarette is not someone, as I think you called it, 'in the system,' right?" Les asked.

"Yes, and that's what makes this case so difficult. Let me tell you some other things I found out today. I think I mentioned I attended the police academy many years ago and met a man who became a good friend. I think I also told you he was going to see what he could find out about Pia's ex-husband, Frank Marshall."

"He's the one who jes' got outta prison, right?" Max asked. "Not tellin' ya' yer' business, like I could anyway, but he'd sure be the one I'd go fer."

"Max, I agree with you," Jeff said. "He has what many would consider a motive in that his wife divorced him. Plus, hate to say it, but when a man has been convicted of a crime in the past, statistically he's far more likely to commit another crime than someone who's never been convicted."

"Hold everything for a minute," Marty said. "I want to get a pad of paper and make some notes. Seems like there's more and more people and evidence. Don't say anything until I get back." She returned a moment later and sat down at the table, pen and pad of paper in front of her.

"Jeff, you can go on now. I'm just going to write a couple of things down."

"Max, back to Frank Marshall. Even though he'd seem to be a prime suspect, his fingerprints are in the system, and they don't match the ones on the cigarette or on that piece of newspaper. That's a major problem."

"You know art's my thing," Les said, "not crime, but isn't there a chance that the piece of newspaper and the cigarette are unrelated to the crime. I know it looks like they're part of it, and the cigarette had Pia's DNA on it, but what if someone picked the cigarette up intending to smoke it since very little of it was gone? What if the newspaper clipping was from someone who was just doodling on it, not specifically targeting Pia by drawing a red circle around her photograph? In that case, couldn't it have been Frank?"

Jeff was quiet for a long time and then he answered Les. "Theoretically, yes, those things could have happened, and Frank could be the murderer. That would fall into the area of nothing more than coincidences, and I'm not a big fan of coincidences. Here's something else.

"My friend went to Frank's apartment and talked to him this afternoon. He told Frank he was helping the Palm Springs Police Department with a murder case regarding his ex-wife. He said Frank's eyes were red, and it looked like he'd been crying ever since he'd found out Pia was dead. He told my friend he knew the police would turn up sooner or later and that he'd be a suspect because of his past."

"I don't know," John said. "Even if he denied it, and since you haven't mentioned he was arrested, I'd still think he was the murderer."

"Hear me out, John. Frank told my friend he'd thought about going to Palm Springs to see the man his ex-wife was going to marry, but he couldn't find a car to borrow and he doesn't have enough money to buy one. He said he could prove he was in Los Angeles the evening Pia was murdered, because he'd bought cigarettes at a convenience store not far from his apartment, and he was sure the clerk would remember him. Evidently the clerk's wife was in the store with their baby, and the couple and Frank talked for a long time about how Frank was sorry he'd never had children."

"Get out the violin, Jeff. My heartstrings are bleeding," John said.

"Well, they might be, but not only did the clerk corroborate Frank's story and the time he'd been in the store, but he gave my friend a copy of the security video that recorded each person who came into the store as well as the date and time they entered and left. The video clearly shows Frank was in the store from 8:05 until 8:12 on the night Pia was murdered. Frank was definitely in Los Angeles when Pia was killed. We know she was murdered between 7:30 and 8:30 that night. I talked to her just before 7:30 when she went outside to smoke a cigarette, and her body was discovered just before 8:30.

That's all solid."

"Sure would make it easier if it hadda been him. The less ex-felons we got roamin' the streets, the better off we'd all be," Max said, the redneck in him being fully aroused.

"All right, Jeff. I've got Frank written down, and I can cross a line through his name, because according to what your friend found out, there's no way he could be the murderer," Marty said

"That's true, Marty. John, if you don't mind, how about putting a little more wine in my glass, would you? Thanks. All this talking makes me thirsty," he said grinning.

Jeff held out his glass to John and resumed talking. "If you remember, last night I mentioned a man by the name of Luigi Marco and his tie to a presumed Mafia man by the name of Roberto Battisto. My friend was able to trace Luigi to a restaurant that's owned by Roberto Battisto. It caters to the entertainment industry. Evidently Luigi is someone who does whatever Battisto needs doing. My friend was able to talk to him."

"I don't quite understand what a Mafia man has to do with Pia Marshall. I must be missing something," Marty said.

"Stay with me. I'll get there," Jeff said. "Luigi has been in jail a couple of times for some misdemeanors. He had a good lawyer and was always able to beat the rap on other more serious charges. That means his prints are in the system, and they don't match the ones on the cigarette or the newspaper clipping. Here's what's interesting. He said he'd attended the cocktail party on behalf of Roberto Battisto because Battisto was thinking about possibly investing in Jack's polo team."

"Are you thinking money laundering?" Les asked. "I've read that Mafia people often do that."

"Possibly, but I don't think that's why Luigi was sent there by Battisto. It turns out Battisto was dating Pia Marshall up until she met

Jack. From what my friend found out Battisto liked her a lot. I don't know how much you know about the Mafia, but having one of their members spurned by a woman is not looked on kindly by the Family. My friend had a hunch Luigi was sent by Battisto to check out Jack. He also wondered if Luigi had been sent by Battisto to take care of Pia, so Battisto wouldn't look like a fool when she married Jack."

"Seems like a stretch, Jeff. I've read a lot about the Mafia, but quite frankly, I always thought the things that were written about them were more about selling books and newspapers than the truth," Marty said.

"I wish you were right, Sweetheart, but unfortunately you're not. There is a code they live by and unless a Mafia member wants to be killed, he has to uphold that code. One of the things in the unwritten code is that a Mafia man is never made to look like a fool by a woman."

"Wait a minute, Jeff. Do you really think Battisto might have sent Luigi to kill Pia?" Les asked.

"I'm saying that might have been why he was sent to Jack's cocktail party by Battisto, but we'll never know. My friend got Luigi to admit he'd stepped outside the barn for a cigarette and saw Pia lying on the ground. He was pretty sure she'd been murdered and decided he better get out of there before he became a suspect, because he knew with his record he'd definitely be a suspect."

"I thought you interviewed everyone who was at the cocktail party the night of the murder," Marty said.

"Correction. We interviewed everyone who was still at the cocktail party the night of the murder. Luigi was not interviewed, because he wasn't there. He left early. There is absolutely nothing to link him to the murder. There's no match on fingerprints, no witness, nothing. I think he was probably telling the truth."

"Well, what about Battisto's involvement? Can ya' do somethin' about him? Like maybe he was behind it," Max said.

"No, I don't think there's anything that can be done. Battisto may have sent him there to murder Pia, but without some type of evidence, proof, or whatever you want to call it, Luigi has to pretty much be taken at his word. Anyway, if he were prosecuted because of our Mafia theory and Battisto was also prosecuted, any good attorney would make sure that the case was thrown out of court. And believe me, he'd be represented by the best attorney the Mafia could buy."

"Jeff, once again I'm fascinated by this stuff," John said. "Tell you what, Max and I had a late afternoon catering job at a large accounting firm in the Springs. We made a ton of sandwiches, and I decided to make some extras for dinner tonight. Why don't Max and I get them and some potato salad, and then we'll continue the conversation?"

"Sounds good. We could probably all use a break. Marty, I see you crossed Luigi off your list. We'll continue after dinner," Jeff said.

CHAPTER TWENTY-TWO

"That hit the spot, John," Laura said. "Sometimes there's nothing more satisfying than a good old-fashioned sandwich with potato salad. Jeff, we had a bite of the peanut butter cookies Marty brought home for you, but I'm wondering if you'd care to share the rest of them with us. A little sweet would finish the meal off perfectly for me!" Before Jeff could respond Marty grabbed the sack of cookies and passed it over to Laura, ignoring the glaring look Jeff was giving her.

"Okay, Jeff, what's next? Did you ever check on Jack's fingerprints?" Les asked.

"Yes. When he was getting ready to open up the polo club, he was fingerprinted. It's part of the California Horse Racing Commission's rules. There was no match for his fingerprints, so that's another dead end, and I have to say, I'm not surprised. Marty, put his name down and then put a line through it," he said laughing.

"You haven't mentioned Kevin Sanders tonight," Marty said. "Find out anything about him?"

"He's another one you can put on your list and cross off, pretty much for the same reason as Jack. Years ago he was fingerprinted because of his polo involvement, and there's no match. He was there the night of the murder, but we have nothing linking him to it. I suppose if we were to speculate, we could say he wanted to get back at Jack by killing Pia, but there isn't one shred of evidence linking him to the murder. What we pretty much have is a lot of people with motives, but not one of them has a direct link to the murder. In other words, plenty of speculation, and not a shred of evidence."

Marty wrote down the name of Kevin Sanders and then drew a line through it.

"Jeff, you haven't mentioned Pia's sister, Gerta Martelli. Any fingerprints for her?" Laura asked.

"I didn't mention her because I haven't been able to get an answer on fingerprints for her. She's a teacher, and while here in California teachers have to be fingerprinted, I don't know what the practice is in New Jersey where she teaches. I was able to find out what district her school's in, but evidently they have an annual three day break this time of year, which may be why she came out here. I don't know why or what the break is attached to, but there's been no answer either at the district office or at her school. I did find out they'll be back in session tomorrow. I hope to have an answer in the morning. Other than that, I'm out of suspects. Do any of you have some brilliant thoughts you'd like to share with me?" Jeff asked looking at the others.

They shook their heads, indicating no. He turned to Laura and asked, "Based on everything you've heard tonight, are you getting any psychic feelings as to who the murderer might be?"

"No. Everything you've said tonight pretty much backs up what I already told you. I still have a sense of feminine energy surrounding the murder, and I don't think it's the feminine energy coming from Pia. I'll be interested to see what happens tomorrow when you finally connect with the school district."

"Me too. If I find out teachers are required to be fingerprinted, I can get in touch with the local police force in New Jersey. In a perfect world I could send the prints from the cigarette and the piece of newspaper to their lab, and they'd have an immediate answer as to whether or not the prints matched Gerta's."

"Well, if they did, then what?" Les asked.

Jeff ran his hands over his face clearly frustrated and tired. "I'd talk to my captain and try to convince him that the matching fingerprints are enough evidence for us to arrest her. We'd have to arrange her arrest through the police in the suburb where she lives outside of Trenton. I'd probably have to travel there and bring her back. If all that happens, there can still be a problem with the police in a small town. They often feel like the big city cops are upstaging them. We've had problems before when the suspect is from a small town in another state."

"Okay, my friends, on that note I think it's time we wrap it up for tonight. I have a couple of hours of research ahead of me. See you in the morning," Marty said. The others followed and soon the compound became quiet as the courtyard lights were turned off for the night.

*****

Marty spent several hours on her computer checking out comparable prices for the pieces she'd appraised in the art glass collection. A few years ago when the auction houses began charging for people to see what the auction items had actually sold for she'd gladly paid the fee, figuring the cost was well worth the time and effort she would have otherwise had to spend researching them.

Although it was time-consuming, she was able to substantiate the values she was placing on the items by what other similar pieces by the artist or company had sold for. In each case the pieces in Pia's collection were far better in quality than other similar pieces that had been sold. In many cases, they were one of a kind, and therefore somewhat priceless. Once again she hoped the appraisal would never need to be used because of theft, breakage, or a fire. They really were unique items.

Now that the hard work of determining the values to be placed on the pieces was finished, she needed to dictate the description, condition, and value of each piece. Carl, a friend of hers in the Palm Springs Appraisal Society, had recommended a woman who typed his appraisals. Marty had developed an excellent relationship with her, and she'd typed up all of Marty's appraisals ever since Marty had begun appraising in the Palm Springs area. Although Marty knew she was tight on time, she was too tired to dictate the report right then. She emailed Janelle, the typist, and asked about her availability for the next few days, because she had a rush project of one hundred twenty-three items.

Within minutes she received a return email from Janelle stating that she'd put Marty's appraisal at the top of her list, and she could have it for her within forty-eight hours. Marty thanked her and wrote back that she'd get it to her within the next couple of days. She took Duke out for his late night walk and then got into bed next to Jeff, whose breathing bordered on being a slight snore but not enough to keep her from quickly falling asleep.

CHAPTER TWENTY-THREE

When Marty woke up Thursday morning she found a note from Jeff. "Good morning, my beautiful wife. I wanted to get to the station early and call the school district in New Jersey, since there's a three-hour time difference. I just want to let you know how much I love you, and I'll see you tonight. Have a wonderful day."

She smiled thinking how lucky she was to have found and married such a wonderful man in her mid-life years. Between Jeff, her appraisal work, and her friends at the compound, she wasn't sure life could get much better. She made a pot of coffee and took Duke out for his morning walk.

As she often did, she used Duke as a sounding board on her walks with him and this morning was no different. "Duke, it's almost like there's something I should be doing, but I don't know what it is. Something's flitting around my brain, but it hasn't landed yet."

He looked up at her quizzically as if to say, "And you're asking me? As if I'd know."

"Duke, I know you don't know what I'm talking about, but let me talk it out. Maybe something will come to me. Thanks for being such a good listener."

Marty saw a car coming towards the compound, and she waved at

Yolanda, the housekeeper who came every other week to clean the four houses in the compound.

Sure would make my life more difficult if I had to clean the house and try to get an appraisal out on a rush basis, she thought. *I imagine the same thought has occurred to Jack. If he didn't have Lupe to take care of everything his life would be even more difficult.*

She continued to talk to Duke and then she stopped suddenly while Duke kept walking. Her arm was painfully jerked from the strain of him pulling on his leash. "I knew I was missing something, and that's it. Come on, Duke, let's go back. We've all missed the most obvious thing." She hurried back to the compound and walked through the gate, carefully latching it behind her, although since Duke never ventured out into the desert without his booties, she realized she was probably being overly cautious.

Marty changed into jeans and a blouse. When she first became an appraiser she'd worn dresses and skirts. She quickly found that as much bending over and reaching up as she was required to do while conducting an appraisal, those types of clothes simply did not work well at all. Slacks became her uniform, and when she'd moved to Palm Springs she exchanged the slacks for jeans. People dressed casually in the resort area, and she was more than happy to follow their lead.

Marty was just gathering up her appraisal equipment when there was a knock on the door. "Come in," she said, expecting to see Yolanda. Instead Laura walked in with a worried look on her face. "Laura, what's wrong? I can see something's bothering you. What is it?"

"I know you respect my whatever it is I have, you know, my psychic abilities. We've talked about it often enough over the years. I have a favor to ask of you. Please don't go to your appraisal today."

"Laura, I can't do that. You know how important it is that I finish up this appraisal so I have time to do the work on the art glass appraisal. I've even arranged for Earl Mathers, the guy that's the expert on antique books, to meet me there this afternoon. Your boss would be furious if I didn't show up. What makes you say something like that?"

"I had a dream last night. You were in the Polo House, and you were in danger, a great deal of danger. I could feel feminine energy surrounding you. I don't know what it's about, but please stay home today."

"Laura, I think you're worrying unnecessarily, but I'll be extra careful today, I promise."

Laura sighed and said, "I was afraid you'd say that. Do me a favor. I know you have a gun. Would you take it and keep it with you today as a favor to me? I still don't want you to go, but if I know you have a gun, at least I'll feel a little better."

"As a favor to you, I will." She walked over to her desk and opened the drawer where she kept it. She unlatched her purse and dropped it in. "There, that should make you feel better."

"Well, I suppose it's better than nothing," Laura grumbled. "See you tonight, I hope." She walked towards the door.

"What's that supposed to mean?" Marty asked. "Not a very optimistic thing to say to your sister."

"May not be. Think about it. There's already been one murder at the Polo House. I don't want you to be the second one."

"My dear sister, I have no intention of being murdered. Before you know it I'll be back here and finished with the appraisal. We'll have our usual glass of wine in the courtyard and a fabulous dinner courtesy of John. Life will be good. You'll see," she said to Laura's back as she was leaving to walk back to her own house.

There's no way I'm going to share my plans for today with her. She'd probably tie me up and lock me in her house until Jeff came home. No, I've got a murder to solve today, and I have a pretty good idea how to find out for sure who did it.

CHAPTER TWENTY-FOUR

Marty pulled up in front of the Polo House promptly at ten o'clock, once again enchanted by the beauty of the large desert home. She rang the doorbell, and in a moment it was opened by Lupe.

"Good morning, Lupe, how are you today?" Marty looked at her and thought she looked like she was in pain.

"Except for the headache I have, I'm fine, but with all the aspirin I've taken I'm sure it will soon be better. Will you be finishing up your appraisal today?"

"I hope so. I only have three areas of the house left to appraise, Mr. Rutledge's office, his suite, and Pia's suite. There will be another appraiser coming this afternoon to look at the antique books. His name is Earl Mathers."

"I'm glad you told me. Mr. Rutledge asked me to get a few things for him at the store. I'll plan on doing that later this morning, so I'll be here when Mr. Mathers arrives."

"That's not necessary. I can let him in."

"No. One of the things Mr. Rutledge feels very strongly about is that everything associated with the polo club have a professional image. That was one of the first things he told me when I started working for him. Anyway, I think he's feeling much better, and he seems to finally be getting over Mrs. Marshall's death, which is a good thing."

Finally getting over Mrs. Marshall's death? In only a couple of days? Is this woman dealing with reality or is she living on some planet I'm not on? Marty thought.

"Excuse me, Lupe, I need to get started in order to finish today. When you see Mr. Rutledge, please tell him I'll be doing his office first and then the two suites. I'll see you later." Marty walked down the hall to Jack's office and put her purse and appraisal equipment on the floor inside the door.

Marty had decided earlier in the morning what she had to do if Lupe left the house. The thought of what she was about to do sent a cold shiver of fear down her back. It helped to ease her nervous tension by keeping busy. For the next hour Marty took dimensions, photos, and made notes as to the condition of the things she was inspecting. She'd need that information when she dictated the report. She heard a car pulling out of the garage and saw Lupe backing down the driveway. She listened for a moment, and the only sounds she heard were the voices coming from Taffy's television in the kitchen.

Marty walked down the hall to the living room and opened the French doors which led to the back yard. To her right was the three car garage, and she saw Lupe's apartment directly behind it. She looked around, but didn't see any gardeners or anyone else in the back yard. She quickly walked towards Lupe's apartment, hoping against hope she hadn't locked the door.

Lupe's white adobe apartment with its red-tiled roof matched the Polo House and looked like a guest house. It could easily be used for if it wasn't being occupied by a live-in housekeeper. The back of the apartment shared a common wall with the rear of the garage.

Although her heart was beating wildly, Marty steeled herself to calmly open the door as if she knew it was unlocked. She didn't know what she'd do if Lupe returned and hoped against hope she'd be long gone from Lupe's apartment before she did return. The door was unlocked, and she walked in. Marty looked around at the comfortable room. Although it hadn't been furnished in the Arts and Crafts style as the Polo House had been, it had a warm feel to it. She took a few steps down the hall and saw the bathroom and the bedroom. Marty assumed the brightly colored serapes hanging on the walls throughout the apartment were reminders to Lupe of her Mexican heritage.

Between the bathroom and what looked like Lupe's bedroom was a closed door which piqued Marty's curiosity. Even though she knew there was a possibility that Lupe wouldn't be gone too long, she couldn't help herself. She had to know what was behind the closed door. She listened for any sounds that would indicate there was a human or an animal behind the door. She heard nothing and gingerly opened the door. She stood stock still, shocked at the sight in front of her. Although the window was closed and a black-out shade had been hung over it, with the natural light coming in from the hall she could clearly see what was in the room.

Every inch of wall surface had been covered with photos of Jack Rutledge and articles about him. There were several photographs of Lupe and Jack. There was an empty L shaped space on one wall, and Marty was certain that the newspaper clipping Taffy had found attached to the back of the cupboard door had been pinned to the wall in that empty space. The shapes matched perfectly. An altar of sorts was on the back wall with a large picture of Jack in the center. It consisted of a tall table with small vases of flowers and candles on it. In front of the makeshift altar was a meditation pillow resting on a small rug.

Taffy told me she was certain Lupe was in love with Jack Rutledge, and from what I'm seeing, I have to agree with her. The articles, the pictures, the altar - this is a room dedicated to Jack Rutledge. Wow! Wait until I tell Jeff about this. It makes perfect sense that Lupe would want to murder Pia to keep Jack from getting married. The only problem is this shrine she's built to honor Jack still doesn't prove Lupe was the murderer, and I'm sure it wouldn't stand up in court.

She stood for several moments looking around the room which paid homage to the man Lupe evidently loved. Marty knew she had to think of something that would tie Lupe to the murder when the word "fingerprints" popped into her mind. She was sure the hunch she'd had that morning when she was on her walk with Duke was correct. Now she needed to get something with Lupe's fingerprints on it and take it to Jeff, so he could have the police lab analyze it.

Marty knew whatever she took from the apartment had to have Lupe's fingerprints on it, but only Lupe's. She had no idea if anyone else was ever in Lupe's apartment. On her way down the hall she passed by the bathroom and thought, *Of course. No one else would use her toothbrush. That would have to have her fingerprints on it.*

When she'd left her house that morning Marty had put a couple of small plastic bags in her pocket, not quite certain what she'd use them for, but knowing they might come in handy. She took a piece of Kleenex that was on the bathroom counter, picked up Lupe's toothbrush, and put it in a plastic bag. Even though she'd felt foolish, she'd brought her purse with her to the apartment, because she'd promised Laura she'd keep the gun Jeff had given her some time ago close to her today. She put the plastic bag in her purse and opened the door to the apartment. She didn't see anyone and began walking towards the main house.

"Good morning, Marty," she heard Jack's booming voice saying. "Did you find something to appraise out here?" he asked.

"No," she said laughing. "It's an old habit of mine to always check out the back of houses and yards in case there's something of value there the owners have overlooked. You'd be surprised what people use as planters, but in your case, I didn't find anything. My husband said he'd treat me to lunch today if I thought I was far enough along in the appraisal to justify it. My friend won't be here until two this afternoon to appraise your book collection, so I'm going to take a little break and meet Jeff. Is that okay?"

"Of course. As hard as you've been working this week, you deserve it. Enjoy your lunch. See you later."

She walked around the house to where her car was parked, got in, and headed for the police station.

CHAPTER TWENTY-FIVE

On the way to the police station, Marty called Jeff. He answered on the first ring. "Sorry I couldn't stick around this morning, but I needed to make that call to the school district back in New Jersey."

She interrupted him, "Jeff, I want to hear all about it. I'm on my way to the station. We've met at the coffee shop next to the station before. Can you meet me there in five minutes?"

He was quiet for a moment and then he said, "Somehow, this worries me. Yes, I'll be there. Anything you want to tell me now?"

"No. See you shortly."

When she pulled up in front of the coffee shop he was crossing the parking lot from the police station. He walked over to her car and opened the door. "Want to stay in here and talk, or do you want to go in the coffee shop?" he asked.

"I can't eat. I'm too nervous, but I sure could use a cup of coffee."

He looked down at her curiously. "Let's go."

After they'd given their order to the perky young barista in the red-striped uniform, he said, "Marty, what's going on? Coming here for the second day in a row is completely unlike you. What couldn't hold until tonight?"

She took the plastic bag containing the toothbrush out of her purse and handed it to him. "Jeff, this is from Lupe's apartment. I went there a little while ago. She has a room in it that's covered with photos and articles about Jack. There was an empty space on one of the walls shaped like an L, and I'm sure that's where the newspaper clipping came from that had Pia's photograph with the red circle around it and the slash mark through it. The room was like a shrine to Jack. It even had what I'd call an altar in it."

"Marty, what made you take the toothbrush?"

"I'm sure Lupe's the one who killed Pia. It all makes sense. I was walking Duke this morning, and I saw Yolanda, and everything fit."

"Marty, I am definitely missing something here. What does Yolanda have to do with any of this?"

"Well, she doesn't really. See, I was talking to Duke, trying to sort out something in my mind."

"Wait a minute. You actually were talking to Duke? Don't you think that's a little unusual?"

"Jeff, quit analyzing me and just listen. Anyway, when I saw Yolanda in her car coming to the compound, I thought of Lupe, because they're both Mexican housekeepers. When I thought of Lupe I remembered what Taffy had said about her being in love with Jack, her headaches, and that Taffy thought Lupe had been acting stranger and stranger. I also thought about the feminine energy that Laura kept referring to. See it all fits. That is, unless you have a match with Gerta's fingerprints. What happened with that?" she asked, picking up the cup of coffee the barista had placed in front of her and taking a sip.

"It's another dead end," he said grimly. "The school district does fingerprint their teachers, and hers was on record. I sent the fingerprints from the piece of newspaper and the cigarette to the New Jersey State Police. They're the agency that stores the fingerprints. Anyway it was a big fat no match. Maybe you're onto something. Maybe it was Lupe. I'll take this toothbrush over to the crime lab and see what they can come up with."

"Good. I'm glad I thought to do it, although I have to admit my heart was in my throat the whole time I was in her apartment. I kept thinking what would happen if she came back early."

"Marty, if you're right about this and Lupe is the murderer, you could be in a great deal of danger. When you go back to the Polo House, I want you to act very normal and don't give Lupe any reason to suspect you think she might be the murderer. Will you promise me that?"

"I'll do you one better, Jeff. Laura had one of her flashes from wherever in a dream last night and thought I could be in danger today. She wanted me to stay home and not go to the Polo House. I told her that was an impossibility, but she made me promise I'd take my gun with me." She opened her purse and showed it to him. "See, I'll be just fine. Don't worry."

"I'm worried. If Laura said you could be in danger that really concerns me. I'll be so glad when you're finished with this appraisal, and you're safely at home." He put several dollar bills on the table and said, "Hate to run, but I want to see what the crime lab can find out from these prints. I'll either call you or let you know tonight."

"I need to get back, too. Earl Mathers will be at the Polo House pretty soon to appraise some of the antique books in Jack's library. I need to show him which ones, although since that's his specialty I'm sure he'll know what's worth appraising and what isn't. Even though his name will be on the book portion of the appraisal, my name is the final one on it. See you tonight."

CHAPTER TWENTY-SIX

Promptly at two that afternoon the doorbell rang at the Polo House. Marty heard Lupe's voice ask someone in and assumed it was Earl. A moment later there was a knock on the doorframe of the library and Lupe said, "Mrs. Combs, your friend is here."

"Thanks, Lupe." Marty noticed that Lupe's right eye was twitching, and she wondered if she was having one of her headaches. Then she noticed that Lupe was grinning for no apparent reason. "Lupe, did I miss something? I can't help but notice that big smile."

"No, Mrs. Combs. I'm just happy that things are getting back to normal around here. If either of you need anything, let me know. I think you finished with Mr. Rutledge's office. He told me he was going to be in there most of the afternoon, trying to catch up on things."

"We'll be fine," Marty said. *Things are getting back to normal around here? I haven't been around Lupe very long, but I wonder if she's all right. She seems a lot different today than she was when I first met her on Monday. I wonder if she has some type of mental disorder that's associated with her headaches, and it's getting worse.*

"Earl, the books I want you to appraise are here in the library. As I told you when I talked to you on the phone, there are a number of antique books as well as contemporary ones. Don't bother with the contemporary ones. You'll have your hands full just appraising the antique ones. I'm almost finished with Mr. Rutledge's suite, and the only thing I have left to do is the other suite."

Marty didn't know if Earl was aware a woman had recently been murdered on the premises, but decided there was no reason to bring it up, since it wasn't relevant to his book appraisal. She walked back to Jack's suite and picked up where she'd left off. An hour later she started to walk down the hall to what had been Pia's suite. When she was in the hall she thought she heard raised voices coming from Jack's office. She set her purse and the appraisal equipment down on the floor of the hall. Evidently she wasn't the only one to hear the voices, because she almost collided with Taffy as she came out of the kitchen.

"Taffy, what's going on?" Marty whispered.

"I have no idea," she answered whispering back. "I turned off the television, because I didn't like the program that was on, and I heard raised voices coming from Mr. Rutledge's office."

They quietly walked in the direction of Jack's office. They stopped just short of the open door leading to the office and as they got closer, heard Lupe say, "Mr. Rutledge, don't tell me you don't love me. I know you do. It's a good thing I killed that Pia woman. You were too good for her. We can live here, and I promise I'll make you happy. I know what you like. She didn't know anything about you. I've been with you for ten years. We're going to be so happy together," she said in a voice that sounded maniacal.

"Lupe, are you telling me you're the one who murdered Pia? Is that what you're saying?" Jack asked in a raised voice filled with both shock and anger.

"Mr. Rutledge, it's not as if I haven't noticed the looks you give me when you think no one else is looking. I know you want to be with me as much as I want to be with you. I know that woman cast some kind of a spell on you, but I broke the spell when I killed her. I can tell you're already becoming happier now that she's gone. You're free to be with me."

"You're crazy," Jack yelled as he stood up and walked around the desk toward Lupe. As he started to approach her, Lupe's primal survival instinct kicked in, and she took two long strides and opened one of the drawers on Jack's desk.

Marty and Taffy were standing next to the open doorway and looked at each other with horrified expressions on their faces. Marty sensed some movement next to her, turned, and to her surprise realized that Jeff and another policeman were standing next to her, the two of them having quietly crept into the house. Both of them had their guns drawn.

Lupe pulled a gun from the desk drawer and pointed it at Jack. "No, I'm not crazy, but if you won't be with me, I won't let you be with anyone else," she said cocking the hammer on the pistol. "Remember how you insisted all of your employees know how to shoot a gun, because you were worried someone would try and break into the house and steal your art pottery collection? You probably never thought your gun would be the thing that would kill you, did you?" she asked, laughing in a deranged way.

Suddenly there was a gunshot, and Lupe fell to the floor screaming that she'd been shot. Her gun slid across the highly polished tile floor and came to a stop at Jack's feet. Jeff and the other policeman ran into the room. "Police! Lie on your stomach and put your hands behind your back." The other policeman placed handcuffs on Lupe as she lay on the floor, sobbing.

Jack reached down and picked up the gun resting at his feet. "Detective, I've never been so glad to see anyone in my life. I guess she's the murderer. She admitted it to me, and I see your wife and Taffy standing in the doorway. I imagine they heard it as well, is that right?"

"Yes, we were standing outside your office when she admitted it. Jeff, I'm just glad you got here when you did, but how did you know to come?" Marty asked, while a very shaken Taffy sank down in the chair nearest the door.

"First of all, the prints on the toothbrush matched those on the newspaper clipping and the cigarette. When the technician brought me the results I knew Laura had been right in asking you not to come today. The feminine energy wasn't Gerta's, it was Lupe's. All we need to do is get fingerprints from Lupe and match them up to the others. That, along with witnesses hearing Lupe tell Jack she murdered Pia, will be more than enough to send her to prison for a very long time."

"Detective, I'm really confused. I know nothing about a newspaper clipping or a toothbrush. Want to fill me in?" Jack asked.

"Yes, but first I need to call the paramedics and have them transport Lupe to the jail ward of the county hospital. She has a minor gunshot wound to her shoulder that needs to be treated by a doctor."

After the paramedics, accompanied by the policeman that had come to the Polo House with Jeff, had taken Lupe away, Jeff told Jack about the fingerprints, Marty's "aha" moment in the desert, Laura's extra-sensory abilities, and what she'd thought about the case. He told Jack that Marty had really been the one to solve the case, and both the police department and Jack owed her a big thank you. He also told him they would be searching Lupe's computer to see if they could determine if she'd done any research on chloroform.

Marty accepted Jack's thanks with humility and credited Taffy for alerting Marty to Lupe's deteriorating mental condition. Marty could tell that talk of extra-sensory things was beyond Jack's comfort level, and he'd prefer to stick with the things that could be explained by the five senses.

"Jack, I'll be back tomorrow to take a statement from you. Right now I want to get down to the station and fill out the paperwork needed for the District Attorney to charge Lupe with murder and attempted murder." He turned to Marty and said, "You showed me the gun in your purse when we met for coffee a couple of hours ago. Might I suggest in the future if you're going to keep it in your purse that you actually have your purse with you." Jeff said with a raised eyebrow, looking sternly at her.

"Jeff, when I walked out of Jack's suite to go to Pia's suite, the last thing I thought I would need was my gun, so I put my purse and my appraisal equipment on the hall floor. Seriously, if I walked around everywhere in this house with my purse hanging over my shoulder, the staff and Jack would probably have had me committed."

"Marty, we'll discuss this further at another time. I'm going to the station now."

"Okay, I'm pretty shaken up, but I can't leave Earl here, so I might as well finish up the last of the appraisal. See you tonight."

Marty walked into the library to see how Earl was doing. He looked up from the book he was leafing through and said drily, "Marty, did I just hear a gunshot? I don't feel very comfortable doing appraisals when there are gunshots."

"Yes, you did," she said sitting down. "It's over now, but it's been a long week. "Why don't you take a break, and I'll tell you all about it."

CHAPTER TWENTY-SEVEN

When Marty opened the gate to the compound that evening she was immediately surrounded by Laura, Les, John, Max, and of course Duke, who had been patiently waiting for her by the gate.

"I'm so glad you're all right. About three-thirty this afternoon I started feeling great, and I knew you were out of danger," Laura said. "Les had the television on while he was painting, and he saw Jeff entering the police station. The commentator said a woman had been arrested and was being charged with the murder of Pia Marshall. So I was right about the feminine energy?"

"Yes, you were. I'm sure all of you want to hear what happened, but I need to change clothes and walk Duke. I'll be back in a few minutes."

"We knew that's what you'd say, so I walked Duke for you. Guess what? I got him to walk with me in the desert without his booties." Les said.

"Les, you walked him? You never do that, and without his booties? How did you get him to go with you?" Marty asked as she looked at him in amazement.

"I'm the alpha male, and I think he realized it. I simply told him in no uncertain terms that we were going to take a walk in the desert, and he did."

"I can't believe it. Does that mean you're the only one who can walk him without his booties being on? I don't think of myself as being much of an alpha male."

"That's true, Marty, but now maybe you can get Jeff to walk him. I'm sure Duke will think he's the alpha male."

"Enough of this alpha male stuff," John said. "Marty, I'm dying to hear everything. Put your stuff down, and I'll get you a glass of wine. Start talking," he said as he poured her a glass of chardonnay. "By the way, Marty, that's the good stuff. It's Rombauer. I only pour it on special occasions, and I'm gathering this is one of those times."

"So it is, John, so it is. I'm alive. Jeff got there just in the nick of time, and presumably the murderer is now behind bars. Okay, here's what happened…"

She'd just gotten to the part where Jeff shot Lupe when he walked through the gate. Everyone applauded. Jeff leaned down and kissed Marty.

"Since Marty has evidently filled you in on the day's events, I'll finish up by telling you Lupe has been charged with murder, and she's in jail. She'll be arraigned tomorrow. I have a sense she has some type of mental and/or emotional problem. Marty mentioned she had headaches, so I wouldn't be surprised if there wasn't a link between them and her current mental condition. If that's true, and it can be proven she was mentally incapacitated, she won't go to trial."

"Don't quite seem fair," Max said. "She murdered somebody, and she outta go to prison."

"Well, whatever anyone's feelings are regarding that issue, the law is the law, and it clearly states that if someone is mentally incapacitated they can't be tried for a crime they've committed, but I promise you that she will spend a long, long time in a state mental hospital."

"Guys, I'm going to change the subject and talk about food. One of my regular customers at The Red Pony just returned from a fishing trip to British Columbia and gave me a couple of big pieces of salmon he caught while he was there. I thought we'd have eggs benedict tonight only I'm going to use salmon that I'll have Max barbecue instead of ham. Believe me, there is no comparison between farm raised salmon and wild salmon. Have another glass of wine, and we'll be back shortly with dinner."

An hour later after they'd all agreed John had spoiled the traditional style of eggs benedict forever for them, Marty said, "I'm sorry to crash, but I think the events of the day coupled with the late nights I've had to spend researching, have finally caught up with me. I'm turning in. Love you all and see you tomorrow. Duke, why don't you stay here with the alpha males and see which one of them is going to take you out for your walk tonight?" As she stood up, she winked at Les and Jeff, hoping they could convince Duke that he should be bootie free from now on.

RECIPES

NOT YOUR MAMA'S MAC AND CHEESE

Ingredients:
3 ½ tsps. kosher salt (If you don't have it, you can use table salt, although I definitely prefer kosher.)
1 tbsp. vegetable oil
3/4 lb. orecchiette pasta (Sounds exotic, but it's easy to find in the pasta section of your supermarket.)
1 cup whole milk
1 cup cream
3 tbsps. butter
4 tbsps. all-purpose flour
2 cups Gruyere cheese, grated
1 cup extra-sharp Cheddar cheese, grated
¼ tsp. freshly ground black pepper
¼ tsp. cayenne
¼ tsp. freshly grated nutmeg (While I do think freshly grated is better, if you don't have it, you can use nutmeg that's already been grated.)
¾ lb. crab meat (Fresh is best, but pretty hard to find. I did find lump crab meat at a Costco store. You could always substitute another type of seafood, but I'm not a fan of the fake crab meat.)
2 tbsps. fresh chives, finely chopped

NOTE: I've been known to substitute other types of hard cheese if I happen to have some already on hand.

Directions:

Preheat oven to 350 degrees. Add 3 tsps. kosher salt and vegetable oil to a large pot of water. Bring to a boil. Add the pasta and cooked per directions on package, usually around 8 minutes, but do taste it for doneness. Drain in a colander. (It's a thicker pasta than say linguine or fettucine, so you don't want to undercook it.)

While the pasta is cooking, put the milk in a small saucepan and heat but don't boil. Melt the butter in a large Dutch oven type pan and add the flour. Whisk the flour and butter together for 2 minutes. Add the milk to the flour and butter and whisk for 2 more minutes or until smooth and slightly thickened. Turn the heat off.

Add cheese, remaining ½ tsp. salt, pepper, nutmeg, cayenne, seafood, and pasta. Stir to mix well. Transfer to individual gratin dishes or to an 8" x 8" glass baking dish. For gratin dishes, bake for approximately 35 minutes. If using a glass baking dish, bake for 50 minutes. Ovens vary, so check for a little browning on the top.

Garnish with chopped chives and enjoy!

SPINACH, PISTACHIO & PECORINO SALAD

Ingredients:
2 tbsps. Extra-virgin olive oil (As you know, I do think it makes a difference.)
4 tsps. cider vinegar (If you don't have cider vinegar, you can use white wine vinegar.)
½ tsp. honey
1/8 tsp. kosher salt
1/8 tsp. black pepper
½ cup red onion, sliced vertically
¼ cup unsalted pistachios, roasted and chopped (You can also use

walnuts or sliced almonds.)
1 5 oz. package of baby spinach
¼ cup Pecorino Romano cheese, shaved (I use a vegetable peeler.)
4 medium mushroom caps, sliced

Directions:

Whisk first 5 ingredients together in a small bowl. In a separate bowl combine onion, nuts, mushroom slices, and spinach. Add the oil mixture and toss to coat. Sprinkle with cheese. Serve and enjoy!

TOM'S CHILLED CUCUMBER-AVOCADO SOUP

Ingredients:

1 cucumber, peeled and coarsely diced (reserve 2 tbsps. for garnish)
1 avocado, peeled and coarsely diced (reserve 1 tbsp. for garnish)
½ tsp. finely grated lime zest (You can substitute a lemon, but since we have a lime tree that produces and produces, I always use limes.)
1 tbsp. fresh lime juice
¼ cup coarsely chopped fresh cilantro (reserve 1 tbsp. for garnish)
1 large green onion, coarsely chopped
1 jalapeno pepper, seeded and coarsely chopped
1 cup plain yogurt
1 cup cold water
1 ½ tsps. kosher salt
¼ tsp. freshly ground pepper

Directions:

Puree the ingredients and ladle into 4 bowls, garnishing with reserved cucumber and avocado. Cover each bowl with plastic wrap and refrigerate for at least 30 minutes. Garnish with reserved cilantro leaves. Serve and enjoy!

NOTE: I prefer this soup on a hot day. Another reason I like this soup is in addition to the lime tree we have an avocado tree as well as lots of green onions and depending on the season, cucumbers.

LIAM'S PEANUT BUTTER COOKIES

Ingredients:
½ cup granulated sugar
½ cup brown sugar (I prefer to use light brown sugar.)
½ cup peanut butter (Creamy or chunky, your preference.)
¾ cup softened butter
1 egg (I like jumbo eggs.)
1 ¼ cups all-purpose flour
¾ tsp. baking soda
½ tsp. baking powder
¼ tsp. table salt
8 oz. peanut butter chips
2 tbsps. sugar for fork dipping

Directions:
In a large bowl mix the peanut butter, sugars, butter, and egg. Stir in the flour, baking powder, baking soda, and salt. When fully combined, gently stir in the peanut butter chips. Cover and refrigerate for at least two hours.

Heat oven to 375 degrees. Shape dough into balls, approximately 1 ¼ inches. Place about 3 inches apart. Dip a fork in the remaining sugar and flatten the balls, making crisscross patterns.

Bake until light brown, approximately 9 – 10 minutes. Cool for 5 minutes and then transfer to a wire rack. Enjoy!

CHICKEN CORDON BLEU WITH RASPBERRY CHIPOTLE SAUCE

Ingredients:
2 large skinless chicken breasts
12 slices of Black Forest deli ham
4 slices of pepper-jack cheese
½ cup raspberry chipotle sauce (Sometimes I can find it at Costco.

When I can't, I go online and buy it.

Caution: refrigerate after opening, as it's very susceptible to mold if you don't.)
Oil cooking spray
Salt and pepper
Toothpicks

Directions:
Preheat oven to 400 degrees. Cut the chicken breasts in half, widthwise, making 4 chicken breasts. Butterfly each one and lay it open like a book. Make four stacks of 3 pieces of ham and 1 piece of cheese. Tightly roll each one up and place it in the center of a butterflied breast. Fold over the top of the breast to conceal the ham and cheese and secure with toothpicks. Repeat for other 3.

Spray baking dish with oil. Salt and pepper the chicken breasts on both sides and place in dish. Bake for 25 minutes. Heat raspberry sauce in microwave for 2 minutes. Remove the toothpicks, plate chicken breasts, and drizzle sauce over the top. Place extra sauce in a gravy boat to be used as needed. Enjoy!

Kindle & Ebooks for FREE

Go to www.dianneharman.com/freepaperback.html and get your FREE copies of Dianne's books and favorite recipes immediately by signing up for her newsletter.

Once you've signed up for her newsletter you're eligible to win three paperbacks. One lucky winner is picked every week. Hurry before the offer ends!

ABOUT THE AUTHOR

Dianne lives in Huntington Beach, California, with her husband, Tom, a former California State Senator, and her boxer dog, Kelly. Her passions are cooking, reading, and dogs, so whenever she has a little free time, you can either find her in the kitchen, playing with Kelly in the back yard, or curled up with the latest book she's reading.

Her award winning books include:

Cedar Bay Cozy Mystery Series
Kelly's Koffee Shop, Murder at Jade Cove, White Cloud Retreat, Marriage and Murder, Murder in the Pearl District, Murder in Calico Gold, Murder at the Cooking School, Murder in Cuba, Trouble at the Kennel, Murder on the East Coast

Liz Lucas Cozy Mystery Series
Murder in Cottage #6, Murder & Brandy Boy, The Death Card, Murder at The Bed & Breakfast, The Blue Butterfly, Murder at the Big T Lodge

High Desert Cozy Mystery Series
Murder & The Monkey Band, Murder & The Secret Cave, Murdered by Country Music, Murder at the Polo Club

Midwest Cozy Mystery Series
Murdered by Words, Murder at the Clinic

Jack Trout Cozy Mystery Series
Murdered in Argentina

Coyote Series
Blue Coyote Motel, Coyote in Provence, Cornered Coyote

Website: www.dianneharman.com
Blog: www.dianneharman.com/blog
Email: dianne@dianneharman.com

Newsletter
If you would like to be notified of her latest releases please go to www.dianneharman.com and sign up for her newsletter.

CPSIA information can be obtained
at www.ICGtesting.com
Printed in the USA
FSOW01n2032161017
39991FS